A Ticket to Ryde
and Other Stories

Philip Ion

Published by

MELROSE BOOKS

An Imprint of Melrose Press Limited
St Thomas Place, Ely
Cambridgeshire
CB7 4GG, UK
www.melrosebooks.co.uk

FIRST EDITION

Cover designed by David Pearce

ISBN 978-1-908645-70-8

Printed and bound in Great Britain by:
Martins the Printers, Spittal, Berwick upon Tweed

"To my Mum and Dad and all the family,
for always being there for me,
to all the people who have helped and supported me
throughout my education,
and to rail enthusiasts everywhere."

"If a man does not keep pace with his companions, perhaps it is because he hears a different drummer. Let him step to the music which he hears, however measured or far away."
(Henry David Thoreau – author, poet and philosopher, 1817–1862)

"Ah, but a man's reach should exceed his grasp, or what's a heaven for?"
(Robert Browning, 1812–1889)

"There was a rocky valley between Buxton and Bakewell, once upon a time, divine as the vale of Tempe... You Enterprised a Railroad through the valley — you blasted its rocks away... The valley is gone, and the gods with it; and now, every fool in Buxton can be at Bakewell in half-an-hour, and every fool in Bakewell at Buxton; which you think a lucrative process of exchange — you Fools Everywhere."
(John Ruskin, 1819–1900)

CONTENTS

A TICKET TO RYDE – AND BEYOND   1
Chapter 1: The Ambition   3
Chapter 2: Another Idea   5
Chapter 3: Fred, Wight and Bluebell   7
Chapter 4: A Long Walk   13
Chapter 5: Determination – and Disappointment   18
Chapter 6: A Major Rethink   22
Chapter 7: Another Meeting   24
Chapter 8: Construction   27
Chapter 9: The Grand Opening   31
Chapter 10: Reflection   36

A TALE OF TWO REOPENINGS   37
Chapter 1: History of the Woodhead and   39
             Matlock-Buxton Routes
Chapter 2: The Start of Work   44
Chapter 3: Tunnel Troubles   48
Chapter 4: Snow Problems   51
Chapter 5: From Bad to Worse   53
Chapter 6: A Desperate Appeal   56
Chapter 7: Rapid Progress   59
Chapter 8: The Last Chance Saloon   63
Chapter 9: The Acid Test   65
Chapter 10: Homeward Bound   73

THE JINXED RAILWAY   77
Chapter 1: Authorisation   79
Chapter 2: Announcement   82
Chapter 3: Recruitment and Construction   84

Chapter 4: The Grand Opening   88
Chapter 5: The First Problem   91
Chapter 6: Something Fishy   94
Chapter 7: Two More Mishaps   99
Chapter 8: Rock Bottom   103
Chapter 9: The Aftermath   109
Chapter 10: Disaster Averted   113
Chapter 11: The Reward   119

THE RAILWAY ENTERPRISE   **123**
Chapter 1: Alternative Possibilities   125
Chapter 2: Significant Progress   129
Chapter 3: The First Run   136
Chapter 4: The Christmas Rush   147
Chapter 5: Up for the Cup   151
Chapter 6: Olympic Specials   159
Chapter 7: New Developments   162
Chapter 8: Additional Benefits   175
Chapter 9: A Significant Landmark   179
Chapter 10: Theatre Excursion   181
Chapter 11: Queens and Rugby   187

A TICKET TO RYDE
– AND BEYOND

The Isle of Wight Steam Railway have at last realised their ambition of establishing a connection to the Island Line. However, now the Chairman comes up with an even more ambitious proposal – a tunnel to the mainland! Many of his staff think that this idea will be well beyond their means, and it takes some time to convince them.

Eventually, they draw up plans for the new route after negotiating a joint deal with Network Rail, and these are put before the Government. However, the Transport Secretary identifies various problems and the plans are rejected.

Determined not to give up easily, the Chairman vows to redraw the plans, but many of his staff start to lose faith in him after feeling the project is too ambitious and he faces a difficult task to keep them on-side. Will the idea succeed, or will it prove to be a bridge – or rather a tunnel – too far?

CHAPTER 1

THE AMBITION

The railways of the Isle of Wight have always held a particular fascination for enthusiasts. At one time, the island boasted quite an extensive network of lines, many of which are now closed.

Part of the system was in the form of a cross, with Newport – the main town on the island – at its centre. From here, lines ran north to Cowes, west to Yarmouth and Freshwater, east to Ryde and south to Sandown. In addition, there was a line running down the eastern side of the island from Ryde Pier Head via Brading, Sandown and Shanklin to Ventnor. This line also had a branch at Brading to Bembridge, while the Newport-Sandown line had a branch running to Ventnor West.

Alas, the island suffered particularly badly from the 'Beeching Axe' of the 1960s. When attempting to identify hopelessly uneconomic cases as candidates for closure, the Isle of Wight stuck out like a sore thumb – at least 20 stations on the island did not appear to serve anywhere immediately nearby. Consequently, lines on the island began to be closed down, until it eventually became apparent to the people there that the Government ultimately wanted to axe the whole system. At that time, a campaign was mounted to try and save what little was left of it, with the result that an eight-and-a-half mile stretch of line from Ryde to Shanklin was retained. Most of this line has since been singled, with a passing loop at Sandown.

Surprisingly, some time later it was even announced that the line would be electrified. Third rail electrification at 650 V dc was decided on as it was considered to be cheaper, but this presented a problem. Ryde Tunnel, running between the town's Esplanade and St John's Road stations, was prone to flooding, so this meant that the track inside the tunnel would have to be raised in order to keep the conductor rails out of the water. However, this exchanged one problem for another, as standard height trains would then no longer fit through the tunnel. Fortunately, at that time London Transport were in the process of decommissioning some of their older Underground units and six of these were shipped over to the island in time for the 1967 timetable. These trains date back to 1938, putting them as the oldest stock in scheduled operation on the national network and hence effectively making the 'Island Line' a heritage line in its own right!

However, the more traditional form of heritage line on the island is in the Isle of Wight Steam Railway. This runs along five miles of the former Ryde-Newport line, with its western terminus at Wootton. It reopened in 1971 and has progressed in stages ever since. In 1987 Chris Green, then Managing Director of Network SouthEast, promised the IoWSR at the reopening of Havenstreet Station: "We'll build a station at Smallbrook as soon as we see your rails coming round the curve."

And they did! Smallbrook Junction Station opened in 1991 at the site where the lines from Newport and Shanklin to Ryde had once joined – yet there had never previously been a station at that point. The station is unusual because, although there are some stations in the UK with no road access – the most extreme example being Corrour on the West Highland Line, which is ten miles from the nearest road – Smallbrook Junction cannot be reached by any method except by train. Its only purpose is to provide an interchange between the two lines, and consequently it is served by Island Line services only when the IoWSR is open.

The IoWSR have several long-term plans, but the most ambitious of these is to re-establish a physical connection to the Island Line and run their trains over it into Ryde St John's Road. Every heritage line dreams of having a connection to the national network – and the IoWSR is no exception!

CHAPTER 2

ANOTHER IDEA

At long last, the two lines were finally reconnected. The volunteers of the Isle of Wight Steam Railway had been campaigning for this moment for years, and finally they had re-established a physical link with the Ryde-Shanklin line. Some of them were assembled on the platform at Smallbrook Junction watching the new lines being installed.

"Well, boys – we've done it at last!" pronounced Chairman Sean Jenkins.

"Excellent!" added Russell Andrews.

"What next?" asked Larry Hardshot.

"Well, we've got the physical link reinstated, but we'll have to wait a bit," explained Sean. "The station at St John's Road will have to be reconfigured, but once they've done that, we'll be able to run trains into it."

"We'll look forward to that," said Tim Horsforth.

Over the next few days, the lines at St John's Road were rear-ranged according to the plans: the tracks serving the two through platforms, which were to be used by the IoWSR, had to be de-electrified in order to allow people to step onto the track to couple and uncouple the locomotives; the bay platform, which was to be used by Island Line services, was to be converted to a through platform; finally, an extra passing loop had to be installed at Brading, in order to replace the one that would effectively be lost from St John's Road.

Once all this had been done, the team members were sitting in the waiting room at Havenstreet, drinking tea and discussing the reconnection.

"Well, we've achieved what most heritage lines want – a connection to the national network!" remarked Albert Mayflower, the oldest of the men.

"Yeah," agreed Fred Perkins. "Only problem is, the line we've connected to is also isolated! That means we don't really have a proper link."

"Well, let's try and establish one," put in Sean.

"What do you mean?" asked Tim.

"Let's build a tunnel to Portsmouth."

Russell, who had been taking a hearty swig from his mug, choked and spluttered.

"Are you mad?" he asked in disbelief, when he had regained his breath. "We'll never afford that!"

"Not on our own, no," admitted Sean. "However, maybe we can come to a joint agreement with Network Rail. After all, mainline services could use it as well in order to reach the island. It'd be great to give it a connection for the first time."

"Are you sure they'll support it?" asked Russell doubtfully.

"Well, there's only one way to find out!"

The others all looked at each other. This was going to be a very ambitious project indeed. Many heritage lines had tunnels on them, but these were all pre-existing ones; no standard gauge heritage line had ever built a brand new tunnel before, and one on this scale was bound to be very expensive – surely well beyond the means of a volunteer-run organisation.

After the day's work was done, the men said their goodbyes and went their separate ways, still not entirely sure if Sean was being serious.

Chapter 3

FRED, WIGHT AND BLUEBELL

The following morning, Fred was reading the morning newspaper at his home in Newport, when he spotted an interesting article. As he read through it, he became more and more excited, and an idea occurred to him.

A few minutes later, he climbed into his car and quickly drove to Havenstreet Station to meet the others for the start of that day's work on the railway. They were all assembled in the waiting room discussing Sean's idea and how crazy it seemed, when Fred pointed out the article in the paper. The others all found it very interesting and thought that his idea was certainly worth trying, even if it didn't come to anything. At that moment, Sean entered the room.

"Well, good morning, everyone!" he greeted cheerfully.

"Morning," they all replied.

At that point, Fred stood up and approached Sean.

"Here, look at this," he said, pointing to the article in the paper. "It looks like the Bluebell Railway have finally managed to re-establish a connection to the national network – and they've had to overcome all sorts of obstacles to do it! I was thinking that it might be worthwhile paying them a visit sometime to talk about their experiences – see if we can pick up any tips for your idea."

Sean put on his reading glasses and skimmed over the article before replying.

"Well, it might be worth talking to them. After all, they've been going for quite a while – if anyone should know how to do it, they should!"

The others filed out of the waiting room to begin their jobs for the day, while Sean showed the article to Steve Adisham, the Station Master at Havenstreet. Steve was intrigued and thought that visiting the Bluebell Railway would be a good idea. Sean then picked up the phone and made a call to arrange a visit. He explained about their plans, and how the article about the Bluebell had given them the idea. Eventually, everything was arranged and Sean assembled the others at the end of the day.

"Right, everyone. I've spoken to the Bluebell Railway, and they've said we can visit them next week. They certainly seem interested in our idea, so I think it'll go well."

The following week, Fred, Sean and Larry were waiting at Smallbrook Junction for the train to Ryde Pier Head – the first leg of their journey. This part only took a few minutes, and before long they were boarding the ferry at Ryde after leaving the train at the end of the pier. The men sat on the upper deck, watching the seafront disappear behind them while the skyline of Portsmouth started to appear on the opposite horizon.

"Lovely day for a ferry trip!" remarked Fred cheerfully.

"Yeah. Great idea of yours, this!" replied Sean.

After the ferry tied up at the quayside in Portsmouth, the group disembarked and walked across to the city's Harbour Station, where they boarded a train bound for London. After a few minutes, it began to pull out of the station and negotiate its way through the city suburbs before joining the main line just north of Hilsea. It then passed through Havant and began to follow the line towards Guildford.

Eventually, the train stopped at Clapham Junction and the men stepped out onto the platform. After a few minutes, they boarded a train to East Grinstead, which was to be the final leg of the journey before reaching the Bluebell Railway. Once this train reached its destination, the men assembled on the platform.

"Right, here we are. What next?" asked Larry.

"They said they'll meet us at Horsted Keynes, so we need to get the next train there," answered Sean.

At this point, the men proceeded to the Bluebell Railway's dedicated platform at the station – the likes of which the IoWSR now had at St John's Road – and sat down on benches to wait for the next train. After several minutes, it steamed into the station and the men climbed into a compartment and sat down, while the locomotive ran round the train.

As the train whistled and pulled out of the station, they became very excited – they were travelling over the newly-reopened section of line, which had been the most challenging for the Bluebell Railway to reinstate. Although it was only two miles from East Grinstead to the former terminus at Kingscote, it had proved an incredibly difficult two miles. The railway had previously covered this section with a shuttle bus service designed to connect with the trains, but the completion of the line had now rendered this unnecessary. During this first stretch, there was no rhythmic 'clickety-clack' sound from the wheels – so often one of the attractions of heritage lines – owing to the fact that the Bluebell Railway had opted for continuously welded rails on the new section, rather than jointed ones. Since this part of the line ran through a more residential area than the rest of the route, it had been necessary to reduce noise as much as possible.

After stopping at Kingscote, the train continued down the line – the wheels now beating their more familiar sound – and the men watched the scenery rushing past. It was a spectacular sight and they were thoroughly enjoying the journey – that is, until the train entered Sharpthorne Tunnel and the compartment started to fill with smoke because they'd accidentally left the window open!

"W-why didn't you c-close the window?" spluttered Sean.

"S-sorry!" gasped Fred, and he pushed the sash of the window up to keep the smoke out.

They were still coughing and spluttering when the train emerged from the other end of the tunnel, so they opened the window again to let the smoke escape and fanned the air with their hands. The sound of the wheels had again been absent in the tunnel, due to the rails inside it also being continually welded – in this case the reason was to reduce the need for maintenance in the confined space.

Soon the train steamed into Horsted Keynes and stopped at the easternmost platform, which was unusual in that it was a single track with platform faces on both sides! The men exited the train on the side nearest the station building and immediately met the Station Master.

"Good afternoon! How do you do?" asked Sean cordially. "We're from the Isle of Wight Steam Railway – I believe we're expected."

"Yes, good afternoon to you, too!" replied the Station Master. "If you'll just excuse me a minute, I need to get the train on its way."

He blew his whistle and called "Right away!" while waving his flag, and the men watched the train chuff away from the station and into the distance.

"Right, I'm Martin Blackwell, the Station Master. I'll show you around here and then we can talk about everything."

Sean then introduced himself.

"That'll be great. Sorry about us being covered in soot, but *somebody* left the window open when we went into the tunnel!"

Fred blushed at this point, while Martin chuckled.

"Oh dear! Well, never mind – it wouldn't be the first time! Anyway, it all adds to the atmosphere!"

"Yes, indeed," agreed Larry.

The men took in the sight of Horsted Keynes Station for a few moments, admiring the 1930s décor and the way it had been so beautifully preserved. Being much larger than most heritage line stations, it was fascinating to behold and the visitors could understand its great popularity as a filming location. With the Bluebell being an ex-Southern Railway line like the IoWSR, the doors, platform canopies and other station furniture were painted in dark green and cream; it reminded the visitors vaguely of Havenstreet. Eventually, they entered the waiting room and sat down.

"Well, what exactly is it you're planning?" asked Martin.

Sean began to explain.

"Well, like yourselves, we've just re-established a connection with the national network – sort of!"

"Oh right. Sounds interesting. Go on."

"The only thing is – it's to the Ryde-Shanklin line, and there's no link between it and the mainland. What we really want to do is see if we can build a tunnel to link it up. That's obviously going to be an ambitious plan, but given all the obstacles you've had to overcome, we were wondering if you could offer us any advice."

"Blimey, that certainly *is* ambitious!"

At that point, three men entered the room and Martin stood up to greet them. He introduced the IoWSR visitors and explained why they were there and what their plans were. Like Martin, they thought the visitors' plans seemed incredibly ambitious, but were also intrigued by their determination.

"Good afternoon," said the first of the men, shaking Sean's hand. "I'm Nick Kingston."

"I'm Kevin Cotton," added the second.

"And I'm Kenny Tutbury," put in the third. "Welcome to our railway."

The seven men walked back out onto the platform and the Bluebell volunteers took it in turns to recount some of the history of their line's preservation while showing their visitors round t' station. Unusually for a heritage line station, Horsted Keyne' an underpass rather than a footbridge, and the men walked th' this to reach the platform on the other side.

As a small Terrier tank engine chugged through with a stration freight train, the men continued to tell the tale of Bluebell Railway was one of the very earliest railway pre schemes in history, having started running as such in 19(in terms of the date of its inaugural train, the Middle in Leeds had beaten it by just seven weeks to be volunteer-run standard gauge line – and even now still often incorrectly quoted as the first!

"What a pity!" exclaimed Sean, when this issue was mentioned.

"Yeah," sighed Martin. "Still, we may not quite have been the first, but we've certainly come a long way since then! In any case, the Middleton was an industrial line, so we were at least the first passenger line to be preserved!"

"Yeah, that's something," agreed Nick. "Anyway, now we'll show you the line close up. Let's walk alongside it."

"Oh dear," groaned Larry. "Don't tell me we're going to be walking all the way back to East Grinstead!"

"Well, that way we can demonstrate to you what we've done."

CHAPTER 4

A LONG WALK

After changing into walking boots and orange hi-visibility vests, the men walked along the platform and down the ramp to the track-side, where they stepped carefully over the rails before leaving the station yard behind and continuing alongside the main line. As they tramped along the side of the line – occasionally standing aside to let trains go past – the Bluebell volunteers explained various jobs that had needed to be done when the line was rebuilt. Eventually they reached the mouth of Sharpthorne Tunnel, where they stood aside and started to walk towards the side of the cutting.

"Can't we just walk through the tunnel?" asked Larry.

"No," replied Kevin. "It's dark in there, and we haven't got lamps – don't want to risk tripping over anything!"

"Why didn't you bring some? It's going to be really tiring climbing over those hills!"

"Well, at least you're in daylight," Kenny pointed out. "It's not easy walking in the dark."

"At least it'd be flat."

The others were starting to lose patience with Larry, until Sean stepped in.

"Look, we're walking over the hill, OK?" he said with finality.

"Oh, alright then," said Larry reluctantly.

With this, the group scrambled up the cutting to the top of the tunnel and began their arduous walk through the woods, Larry struggling to keep up.

"How much further?" he groaned. "My feet are killing me. Can't we have a rest?"

"There isn't far to go – the rest's all downhill from here back to the line," Martin reassured him.

Sure enough, within a few minutes the men reached the other mouth of the tunnel, at which point Larry, desperate for a rest, promptly sat down defiantly on a log just behind the retaining wall. The others stood admiring the view for a moment, then decided that it probably was time to rest and sat down as well. Barely had they become settled than a train whooshed out of the tunnel – a very spectacular sight from their viewpoint!

"See? That was another reason for not walking through the tunnel – if we'd been in at the same time as that, we'd probably have ended up spluttering smoke again!" Sean observed.

"Yeah," agreed Fred. "What's more, it would've been danger-ous to be in there at the same time. We might've had an accident."

"Not really," explained Martin. "We could've just waited in one of the recesses while it went by."

"Still, better to be safe, eh?" remarked Sean.

"Indeed!" agreed the others.

After resting for a while, the men walked carefully down the cutting to the side of the line and started to make their way towards Kingscote. Just after the tunnel, they saw the site of West Hoathly Station, which had not been reopened with the rest of the line to overcome objections from local residents. Only the platforms were extant, the station buildings having been demolished in 1967. Unlike on the section through the tunnel, the single track at this point had been laid in the middle of the former double-track trackbed instead of to one side, so it was too far from either of the platforms to be able to board or alight from a train at this point! However, in 1992 a run-round loop was installed to the north of the station, which was removed in 1994 following the completion of the extension to Kingscote.

Eventually they reached Kingscote, where they sat down on a bench to rest – Larry almost completely exhausted! Fred and Sean were particularly looking forward to seeing the last section of the line, as they gathered that this had been the biggest challenge of all.

A few minutes later, the men stood up, stretched themselves and started on the final leg of their walk. Just after leaving Kingscote, Martin started an explanation of this part of the project:

"Right. This section was the most difficult to reinstate. Parts of the trackbed had been sold off to various people in previous years – you wouldn't believe the hassle it took to overcome that!"

"I can imagine!" remarked Sean.

"Yeah. But that wasn't the biggest problem. You'll encounter that a bit further on."

When the men reached Imberhorne Cutting a short while later, Martin resumed his speech:

"Here we are. This cutting had been used for landfill, so we had to clear it. This gave us two problems: firstly the possibility of there being toxic waste in the tip, and secondly where to move it to – that was even assuming that the local council agreed to us moving it in the first place!"

The Isle of Wight visitors were intrigued. What a lot of obstacles to overcome!

"How did you solve the problem?" asked Sean.

"Now that's a very interesting story!" said Nick, taking over from Martin. "Our next ambition – albeit in the long term – is to reopen the branch from Horsted Keynes to Ardingly. There used to be a viaduct on it, but it's been demolished and it'd be very expensive to rebuild it as a viaduct. However, we've been using the spoil from this cutting to extend the embankment on either side of the gap!"

"I see!" exclaimed Fred. "Kill two birds with one stone, so to speak!"

"Yes, indeed. It means we'll only have to build a short bridge over the road underneath – much cheaper than rebuilding the viaduct!"

Martin then proceeded to tell the Isle of Wight visitors how one sad consequence of the Bluebell's extension had been the line losing its main selling point as the only major heritage line in Britain to have been entirely steam-operated since opening – something it had managed to keep up because it started running before the end of mainline steam in 1968. This had happened due to the need to use diesel traction to clear the cutting, and on one occasion a chartered passenger train had even visited the line, hauled by a Class 73 electro-diesel locomotive – ironically named *Perseverance*!

"Yes, that was a pity," sighed Nick. "Still, I suppose establishing a connection to the national network effectively means we've ended up exchanging one big selling point for another!"

The men continued on their journey, emerging from the cutting and walking over Imberhorne Viaduct. Martin explained that one other problem had been the need for this structure to have expensive regeneration work carried out, and the Isle of Wight men became more and more impressed by the Bluebell's determination to re-establish a link with the national network. Clearing around 300,000 cubic metres of waste from the cutting had been a race against time, since the railway had agreed a Landfill Tax exemption with the European Union and had needed to clear the cutting before the exemption expired. If the deadline had been missed, the projected cost of the work could have increased from around £2million to nearer £9million, potentially adding years to the timescale for completion.

After such a long walk, the sight of East Grinstead Station was an extremely welcome one, and the men sat down on a bench to wait for the next train. The Isle of Wight visitors were to catch a train back to Clapham Junction before returning to Portsmouth, while the Bluebell team members would be taken back to Horsted Keynes on one of their own services. Once the former arrived in the station, the two sets of men stood up and said their goodbyes.

"Well, thank you so much for a lovely day!" said Sean to Martin, as they shook hands.

"You're welcome – and do come again soon!"

"Yeah, that'd be great. I must say, I'm really impressed with the lengths you've gone to in order to reopen this line. Seems you've moved mountains – literally!"

Martin and the other Bluebell volunteers chuckled.

"Yeah, I suppose that's one way of putting it!" grinned Nick. "Anyway, have a good journey home, and do let us know how you get on with your plan!"

"Will do!" replied Fred cheerfully. "Bye!"

The Isle of Wight volunteers boarded the train that would take them back to Clapham Junction and sat down. After a few minutes, it began to pull out of the station and they waved goodbye to their Bluebell counterparts. It had been an excellent day, and most enlightening – even if it had involved such a tiring walk. As they drifted off to sleep during the return journey, they realised just how much they had to think about. If the Bluebell Railway could show such determination and drive to get linked up properly, why couldn't they?

Chapter 5

DETERMINATION – AND DISAPPOINTMENT

Some days after their visit to the Bluebell Railway, Sean, Larry and Fred were meeting with the rest of the Isle of Wight staff to discuss how best to proceed with their plans. The men who had stayed behind had been equally impressed to learn of the lengths their Sussex counterparts had gone to, and were sure that they could draw inspiration from this show of grit and determination.

"Right," said Sean. "Obviously we all agree that the Bluebell's persistence was gallant and should be admired, but at the same time just because it happened for them it doesn't necessarily mean it'll happen for us. After all, even they effectively had to fund their project on the drip – if we don't want to find ourselves doing the same, we've got to negotiate a joint deal."

"That's true," agreed Russell. "This effectively means building a brand new line."

"In some ways, the Bluebell may as well have been," remarked Fred. "Clearing that tip and all."

"Yeah, but there's a difference between building – or clearing – a cutting, and building a tunnel," Albert pointed out. "This will, of course, have to be a bored tunnel rather than cut and cover, since it's underwater! That certainly makes a difference. What's more, the distance involved is over twice that which the Bluebell had to cover."

The men had held several discussions on the subject already, and they had identified the key stages of developing a plan. Firstly, they would have to decide how to fund the project – how much could they afford to contribute, and could they persuade Network Rail and the Government to cover the rest of the cost? They would also need to put forward a strong economic case for the project – what benefits would it bring to the island?

Over the next few weeks, the IoWSR volunteers discussed their plans in detail; first among themselves, then with Network Rail, with whom they hoped they would be able to come to a joint agreement over funding. Eventually they were satisfied that the plans were ready to be finalised, and it wasn't long before they again found themselves waiting at Smallbrook Junction for a train to Ryde Pier Head. After the ferry to the mainland, they boarded a train at Portsmouth Harbour Station, but this time they would be travelling right into London. Once the train pulled into Waterloo Station, the men walked down the platform and assembled on the concourse.

"Right," said Sean. "Now we need to get over to the Houses of Parliament."

"Are we getting taxis?" asked Russell.

"No, it's a lovely day – let's walk!"

"Oh, no!" groaned Larry.

"Look, it's nowhere near as far as Horsted Keynes to East Grinstead, it should only take us about ten minutes!" Fred responded.

Larry looked set to retort, but the others seemed content to walk and so he kept quiet. The men walked out of the station and began to make their way towards the River Thames, the London Eye towering above them. They crossed Westminster Bridge to reach the Houses of Parliament, where they were to attend a very important meeting with the Government and Network Rail. This was the most crucial stage so far, as it was vital for them to obtain backing for the project. Naturally, they were very nervous. Would they put forward a convincing enough case?

"… and we feel that such a link will provide an excellent boost to the economy of the Isle of Wight, by allowing many more visitors to come to the island, plus National Rail services would be able to use the tunnel as well, thereby ensuring additional benefit all round."

"Thank you, Mr Jenkins," said the Transport Secretary, after Sean had finished speaking. "I can see that you have a very strong ambition to connect the Isle of Wight to the mainland. However, you are a volunteer-run organisation, and it is difficult to see how you can afford to fund such a large scale project."

The Chairman of Network Rail stood up.

"Sir, as you may be aware, we are prepared to fund a large part of this project ourselves, as we feel that we can benefit from it significantly as well. We agree that the Isle of Wight would gain a substantial advantage in having a direct link to the mainland."

"Thank you," the Transport Secretary replied. "Well, that certainly makes a difference. However, there are still many issues to discuss."

The meeting proceeded for another hour or so, while various problems were discussed. Although the IoWSR and Network Rail seemed to have forged a determined partnership in order to fund most of the project, the Government would have to contribute the remainder, and doubts were raised over the benefit-cost ratio. Furthermore, there was the issue of the tunnel being shared by steam and electric trains, and how to overcome this.

Unfortunately, neither the IoWSR nor Network Rail seemed to have thought of this potential problem, but they now realised – all too late – that if steam and electric trains passed each other in the tunnel, the smoke from the former could enter the latter through the windows and make it very unpleasant for passengers. Despite their best efforts to marshal counter-arguments to the Government's doubts, the Transport Secretary eventually rejected the plans on the grounds of uncertainty as to whether this issue could be dealt with satisfactorily.

Disappointed, the IoWSR volunteers trudged back to Waterloo Station, the walk seeming much longer than it had on the way there. With heavy hearts, they boarded the next train back to Portsmouth Harbour.

"I knew this was too ambitious," said Russell heavily.

"Don't be like that," replied Sean reassuringly. "At least Network Rail supported us. We've just got to find a way to solve the problem with the smoke."

"Forget it, mate," Tim sighed, shaking his head. "This just isn't meant to happen."

Larry also looked very pessimistic – always the cynic, he'd been certain that something was going to scupper the project, despite all their careful planning. He, Tim and Russell promptly moved seats, leaving Sean almost alone. Fortunately, Fred and Albert still retained some hope and sat either side of him. Fred put his hand on Sean's forearm and said:

"Look, don't let them get you down. We can still do it – we just need to make a few changes."

"Yeah," agreed Albert. "We'll do it. You see if we don't!"

Sean was reassured by this show of support, and thanked them for it. These three sat together all the way back to Portsmouth, while the others sat on the opposite side of the carriage, determinedly looking away from Sean. He began to feel very worried – the last thing he wanted was for all his staff to turn against him at such a crucial time!

CHAPTER 6

A MAJOR RETHINK

The IoWSR staff's general feeling towards Sean hadn't improved by the following morning. Many of them wouldn't speak to him, so he was finding it very difficult to keep them motivated. Fred and Albert still stuck by him, but they seemed to be the only ones. Even Steve, who hadn't been to the meeting in London, seemed more distant than usual. After contemplating the issue, Sean eventually decided not to inform the Bluebell Railway of their setback, and instead concentrated on revising the plans with Fred and Albert.

"Right," he said to them one day. "One way to make sure that there aren't steam and electric trains in the tunnel at the same time would be to build a twin bore tunnel instead."

"Yeah, I suppose," agreed Albert. "However, a tunnel of this length will have to be properly ventilated. After all, there could still be smoke in it even after a steam train has gone through."

"That's true," remarked Fred. "We need to decide how to solve that issue."

"We certainly do!" added Sean firmly. "If there's even one tiny thing we haven't thought of, then this whole idea will be rejected completely."

Eventually the idea of installing extractor fans in the tunnels came to the men. They reckoned that the time between a steam train travelling through the tunnel and the next electric one following it wouldn't be long enough for the smoke to diffuse out naturally, so the fans would help speed up the process! This certainly seemed an excellent solution, but one that would significantly add to the cost, so they had to decide how to overcome this obstacle. It had already been decided that Network Rail may have to foot the bill for the extra cost of building a twin bore tunnel, as opposed to single bore, so to ask them to pay for the fans as well would probably be pushing their luck!

"I know," said Fred one day. "How about we offer to pay for the fans, on condition that we have running powers into Portsmouth Harbour? We could run trains right through – just like the North Yorkshire Moors Railway do into Whitby!"

"Hmm, it's a possibility," replied Sean. "We'd need to try and arrange some big fundraising campaign or something, though."

"Well, I think it's an excellent idea," pronounced Albert. "After all, I don't fancy the prospect of asking Network Rail to have to cough up more money for the tunnel itself, so this might soften the blow."

The men continued to discuss the idea, trying to anticipate potential problems and how to address them. Running right through to the harbour was bound to prove controversial with some people, and there would be all sorts of issues to resolve.

CHAPTER 7

ANOTHER MEETING

After the disappointment of their previous meeting with the Government, Sean was determined to make a much better fist of trying to convince them to support their project. He, Fred and Albert all redoubled their efforts to find solutions to any potential problems. The revised plans were discussed with Network Rail, who were attracted by the offer to pay for the extractor fans in exchange for running powers into Portsmouth Harbour. Eventually the three men were satisfied that they would be able to put forward a much better case; the problem now was getting the rest of the staff back on side!

"I'm still not sure about this," said Russell doubtfully, when the rest of the staff were informed. "It's still a very ambitious plan."

"This whole thing is a waste of time!" snorted Larry.

"Well, I suppose there's no harm in trying," Tim responded hesitantly.

Following several days of discussion, the IoWSR staff – except for Larry and Steve – found themselves on another train journey to London and at another meeting with the Government. This time Sean explained the revised plans in detail to the Transport Secretary, who was intrigued but still doubtful.

"This is bound to be much more expensive, Mr Jenkins. Are you sure you can afford to fund it?"

"We've come to an agreement," announced the Network Rail Chairman, who then proceeded to explain the deal concerning the extractor fans and the running powers into Portsmouth Harbour.

"Thank you," said the Secretary. "However, if there is a direct rail service from Portsmouth Harbour to the Isle of Wight, what about the ferry to Ryde Pier Head? Will it still be needed, and if not, will the station at the Pier Head be needed either?"

Sean cleared his throat. Having anticipated that running right into the harbour would almost certainly eliminate the need for the Portsmouth-Ryde ferry (and with it, the station at the Pier Head), he had his answer ready:

"Sir, during the summer, people take the train along the pier even if they aren't catching the ferry, so there may still be the demand for at least a summer service along it, whether or not there's still a ferry. After all, people often walk along the pier in one direction and catch the train in the other."

"Maybe, but will there be justification for keeping that section of line just for a summer service?"

"Well, one other idea we have – albeit in the long term – is the possibility of one of the tracks in Ryde Tunnel being de-electrified and re-lowered to enable our trains to run through, allowing us to run to Ryde Pier Head. At the very least, the pier section could be mothballed with that in mind."

The Transport Secretary was intrigued by this idea, and the signs were certainly looking better. Sean was quite keen to stress that the idea of gaining running powers to the Pier Head was very much a long-term ambition and not one that they currently had any firm plans for, but at the same time felt that this justified keeping this section of line open.

"What's more, even if there's no longer any need for a ferry service to and from Portsmouth, there could still be pleasure cruises running from Ryde. The station at the Pier Head would be important for people to connect with those."

"Thank you, Mr Jenkins. Having heard the arguments put forward, I can see that you have made a very convincing case for this project, and I am also impressed with the way you have addressed the particular issues that will be affected by it. As such,

I now feel justified in giving backing to it."

"Thank you, Sir."

The men stood up and shook hands before leaving to walk back to Waterloo Station, their mood a far cry from a few weeks before. If nothing else, this experience had taught them the value of making sure that every possible issue was covered when making plans, and also to think of any possible knock-on effects.

Chapter 8

CONSTRUCTION

After a few final arrangements, construction work on the new tunnel was ready to begin. The section of the Island Line from St John's Road to the Pier Head had to be closed temporarily while the preparatory work at the southern end of Ryde Tunnel was carried out. The twin bores of the new tunnel were to deviate from the existing line in opposite directions just inside the tunnel, before descending further underground and re-aligning with each other – an arrangement which was going to be tricky to build and would require an extremely high degree of precision.

There is a tradition in the tunnelling industry that Tunnel Boring Machines – or 'Moles' – cannot start work until they have been named. A competition had been held to name the ones which were to construct the new tunnel, and after several nominations, the final names chosen were *Fiona*, *Alice*, *Alexandra* and *Bertha*.

Once *Fiona* and *Alice* started burrowing the new tunnel at the Isle of Wight end, the same happened on the mainland with *Alexandra* and *Bertha*. These machines were to be guided by laser techniques in order to ensure that they would meet precisely in the middle: it would be very expensive – and embarrassing! – if they ended up tunnelling past each other!

The IoWSR staff watched as the work commenced, delighted that they had managed to reach this stage.

"Well, this is it!" Sean said excitedly, as the TBMs were positioned – *Fiona* in the northbound bore and *Alice* in the south.

"Yes, indeed!" agreed Fred.

"Well, we're making a start, and that's something," Larry said. "Let's just hope there aren't any setbacks!"

"Yes, let's hope so," added Tim.

Over the next few weeks, the work progressed smoothly. Within a couple of weeks it was advanced enough to allow the section of closed line to reopen, since all the heavy work at the Ryde Tunnel end was completed and any further disruption to services would be minimal. Spoil from the tunnel was removed via construction trains with conveyor belts and loaded into wagons, these trains mostly leaving the tunnel at night to ensure a clear run. Behind these trains came machinery to line the tunnels with concrete, while lighting was installed on the walls.

Six months after construction had started, the IoWSR staff were inside what would become the northbound bore of the tunnel, dressed in orange fluorescent overalls, steel-capped boots and white hard hats, to witness the most significant stage of the construction so far. They had been taken into the tunnel on one of the special construction trains and had enjoyed seeing how the work was progressing: the first mile or so of tunnel was virtually finished, with the concrete lining and lights fully installed and operational; the next portion still had the underneath layer of concrete showing, as the prefabricated slabs had not yet been installed; however, the walls of the last stretch were still bare rock and only had temporary lights fixed to them, which made it much darker. Now they were standing close to the end of the tunnel that had been built so far, separated from a rock wall in front of them by a steel platform.

"This is it!" said Sean excitedly.

"It should only be a few minutes now," added the foreman.

Sure enough, before long a chugging sound was heard from the other side of the wall, followed by the sound of drilling. Dust started to fall from the centre of the wall and seconds later an enormous drill bit poked out and cracks started to appear round the hole.

"Stand back!" ordered the foreman.

The IoWSR staff did as they were told, and the wall of rock on the other side of the platform collapsed before their eyes.

When the dust had settled, they looked ahead to see a machine with its headlamps shining brightly on the other side of where the wall had been, the tunnel made by *Alexandra* stretching behind it into the distance. They had done it! They'd broken through!

"Now that was a spectacular sight!" exclaimed Russell.

"Blimey!" remarked Fred.

"We're through!" cried Albert.

"At last," said Larry.

The construction workers began to take some measurements as the IoWSR staff continued to gaze in amazement; where there had previously been a wall of solid rock, there was now a tunnel. After a few minutes, the foreman stood on the platform to address them:

"The alignments are as follows: three millimetres off line, two millimetres off level."

"That is impressive!" Sean observed in awe. "Such excellent precision."

"Oh dear – have to go back and do it again!" joked Larry.

"No, it's OK," said the foreman. "We can make up for such a small difference by simply smoothing the lining out, then no-one will be able to tell."

"I doubt they'll be able to tell anyway!" laughed Albert.

The volunteers were so impressed by this event that three days later they were able to attend the breakthrough of the second bore, constructed by *Alice* and *Bertha*. This time the accuracy was even greater, with the tunnels being just one millimetre off line and perfectly on level. After this, the lining of the tunnels proceeded steadily, the workers becoming increasingly motivated by the fact that they were getting closer and closer to their goal.

Within another four months the construction was completed, and the power was switched on so that the tracks became live for the first time. Various test runs were conducted to ensure that trains could travel through safely, and also to make sure that the extractor fans worked properly.

In addition, like at Ryde St John's Road, the IoWSR were to be allocated their own dedicated platform at Portsmouth Harbour. The track serving the southernmost platform at the station was de-electrified and a run-round loop installed on it, and eventually the tunnel was ready to open.

Chapter 9

THE GRAND OPENING

Some days later, an enormous crowd had assembled at Portsmouth Harbour Station. A red carpet was laid from the stairs up to the platform edge, at which end there was a red tape stretched between two posts, with a box and a microphone behind it. Across the line there was a banner commemorating the date of the event, behind which stood a special train with a gleaming Stirling Single locomotive at the head.

The crowd applauded as the Mayor of Portsmouth strode along the carpet with his associates, his ceremonial chains shining brightly in the sunlight. When the applause died down, he stood on the box to address them:

"Thank you, thank you. Good morning, everyone. As Mayor, it is a tremendous honour to be part of what is such a historic moment for the city, the Isle of Wight, and for the railways in general. I cannot find words to describe what it means to at last have a direct connection to the island for the first time in history."

He then proceeded to give praise to the grit and determination shown by the IoWSR volunteers, and summarised the problems they had been forced to overcome: how they had needed to sort out the issue with smoke in the tunnel, what would happen to the ferry, whether or not the Ryde Pier Head to Ryde Esplanade section of line would be closed, and a whole lot more. After a lengthy tribute to all this, he finally said, "And so, on behalf of the City of Portsmouth, it gives me great pleasure to declare this tunnel – an extension both to the Isle of Wight Steam Railway and the national network – officially open!"

He took out a pair of scissors and cut the ribbon, at which point the crowd applauded and cheered loudly.

"Right – bring it in!" he called.

He waved at the special train to signal for it to move, and it whistled before slowly starting to chuff towards the station. It broke through the banner, at which point more cheers issued from the crowd, and drew up at the platform. Dressed in his best suit for the occasion, Sean stepped out of one of the carriages and shook hands with the Mayor.

"Good morning, Mr Mayor. Sean Jenkins, Isle of Wight Steam Railway Chairman. It is a pleasure to meet you. Would you like to step inside?"

He held the door of the carriage open.

"Thank you very much," replied the Mayor, boarding the train and sitting down in a seat.

The IoWSR had pulled out all the stops to cater for their important guest; a dining car with real tablecloths and silverware had been used, instead of an ordinary seated carriage, and the staff were all wearing their best clothes. While the locomotive was detached from the train and began to run round it, the Mayor looked around, apparently thoroughly impressed.

The locomotive turned round at the triangular junction that had been constructed at the mouth of the tunnel at Fratton, before running tender-first back to the harbour and coupling up to the train. After this, the Station Master blew a whistle and called "Right Away!" while waving a green flag.

In the cab, Russell sounded his whistle and eased the regulator open the tiniest fraction to start the train moving as gently as possible.

"This is it!" he called to Fred, who had the honour of firing the locomotive on this special run.

"Yeah. Here we go!"

The train chuffed through Portsmouth and Southsea Station

without stopping as it headed towards the tunnel. Many people lined the sides of the cutting and stood on bridges to watch the train steam past, cheering and waving as it did so. Russell slowed the train down to traverse the curve of the triangle, giving a long blast on the whistle before it plunged into the tunnel and out of sight.

"Well, here's the big test!" he said excitedly.

The sound of the pistons at work echoed off the sides of the tunnel as the train travelled through it. Before long, the tunnel began to slope downwards, so Russell shut off the regulator to save steam and wound the reverser about halfway forward in order to control the train's descent. As they were effectively coasting on this stretch, Fred was able to relax because there was not much demand for steam.

Once the tunnel levelled out, however, Russell had to open the regulator out again in order to maintain a steady speed, at which point he wound the reverser back down while Fred resumed shovelling coal into the firebox.

The final portion of the tunnel would be the trickiest for the train to negotiate, and Russell and Fred would need to work as a cohesive team in order to keep it going. Imagine their embarrassment if they got stuck in the tunnel with the Mayor on board! With the pistons making an even greater amount of noise as the train climbed back towards the surface, Russell opened the regulator further and turned the reverser up, while Fred was using all his strength to carry on stoking the fire. Shovelling the coal was hard work, and it wasn't long before he started to tire.

"Oh my word!" he gasped, mopping his sweating brow.

"Keep it up, Fred. We're nearly there!" called Russell encouragingly.

A couple of minutes later, Russell sounded the whistle loudly and the train finally emerged from the southern end of the tunnel – it had taken them nearly a quarter of an hour to traverse the five miles since entering it, and they were relieved to be back out in the open air! Many people were standing above the entrance to the tunnel and had a great vantage point to watch it emerge; they waved and cheered as it passed.

The train stopped at St John's Road to take on water – the platforms here being just as crowded as at Portsmouth Harbour – and then resumed its journey. It rounded the curve at Smallbrook Junction and continued through Ashey before approaching Havenstreet, where Steve was standing on the platform waiting to see the train in.

"Here it comes!" he gasped excitedly.

He waved a red flag a little more vigorously than was necessary as the train neared the platform and it began to slow down.

"Havenstreet Station!" he shouted. "Havenstreet!"

Russell had to stop the train very precisely in order to ensure that the door of the Mayor's carriage was lined up with the red carpet on the platform! The door was opened and the Mayor stepped out and shook hands with Steve, who welcomed him to the station. Sean followed and escorted him into the waiting room, after which Steve began to show their guest round.

Sean was looking round the platform at the train when a familiar-sounding voice called, "Hello!"

It was Martin Blackwell, along with the other people who had shown them round the Bluebell Railway when they had visited.

"Hello there! Great to see you!"

"Yeah, we thought we'd return the favour! Blimey, I thought we'd overcome obstacles, but what you've done is amazing!"

"Yes, we're very proud of what we've achieved. This benefits both us and the national network."

Sean took the visitors into the waiting room and introduced them to the Mayor – and also to the staff who hadn't been on the visit to the Bluebell Railway. They were very impressed by what they saw, and even more impressed when Sean told them about the long-term idea to run trains through to Ryde Pier Head.

Eventually, after a long hard day, it was time for the Mayor to leave. Sean shook hands with him and he climbed back into the carriage. After Steve's whistle, Russell drove the train out of the station and the rest of the staff – and the Bluebell visitors – waved as it disappeared.

"What a day!" said Sean. "I'm ready to go home and have a hot bath now!"

"Me too!" agreed Steve.

"Still, it went very well, and I think the Mayor was impressed," Albert remarked.

The men said their goodbyes to each other and left for their homes.

Chapter 10

REFLECTION

A few days later, the staff were sitting on a bench at Smallbrook Junction, watching a train arrive from London.

"I say," said Albert, "isn't it great that we can now travel directly to London from here?"

"Indeed," agreed Larry. "I will admit, I was highly sceptical about whether or not that tunnel would be a success, but it seems I was proved wrong."

The train then began to pull out of the station as it continued towards the end of its journey to Shanklin.

"Mind you, there is one other thing we could try," put in Sean.

"What's that?" asked Tim, taking a bite out of an apple.

"We could try extending the line to Newport."

"Don't be silly!" said Russell.

"Why not? You thought the tunnel would be too ambitious, but we pulled that off. Why can't we do the same again? It wouldn't be anything like as big a project."

"Sean," replied Fred, "let's settle with what we've got for the moment."

Sean did not reply.

The End

A TALE OF TWO REOPENINGS

At long last, and after many struggles, the Woodhead and Matlock-Buxton railway routes have finally been granted permission for reopening. However, the two projects proceed with highly contrasting fortunes: whereas the Woodhead route progresses without a hitch, the Matlock-Buxton experiences nothing but problems.

Cost overruns, avalanches, collapses and accidents cause a great many local people to begin to lose faith in the viability of the reopening, which had already been doubtful beforehand – and even one of the men working on it is growing increasingly sceptical.

Eventually a desperate appeal needs to be made in order to stop the project from being abandoned, and the men hope the smooth progress of the Woodhead revival will convince the Government to continue to support their own scheme. Will everything turn out in the end?

CHAPTER 1

HISTORY OF THE WOODHEAD AND MATLOCK-BUXTON ROUTES

The Woodhead route, running from Manchester to Sheffield via Gorton, Hyde, Hadfield, Woodhead, Penistone and Stocksbridge, was opened in 1845 by the Sheffield, Ashton and Manchester Railway. This started at Manchester London Road Station (later Piccadilly) and ran into Sheffield Victoria, now closed. The single track tunnel at Woodhead caused much congestion, so it was augmented by a second bore in 1852.

By 1857 the SA&MR had merged with other companies to form the Manchester, Sheffield and Lincolnshire Railway – sometimes sardonically referred to as the 'Mucky, Slow and Lazy'. This company was later to become the Great Central Railway.

In 1923 a major shake-up – known as the 'Regrouping' – occurred with regards to railway companies, where the 150 or so companies that existed at that time were consolidated into what became known as the 'Big Four'. The Great Central was merged with companies such as the Great Northern, North Eastern, Great Eastern and North British, forming the London and North Eastern Railway.

After previous proposals had been rejected on cost grounds, in 1936 it was decided that the Woodhead route should be electrified to save the expense of building more locomotives to assist trains up the gradients. However, the project was suspended during the Second World War and work did not resume until 1946. The tunnels at Woodhead and Thurgoland were discovered to be too low and narrow for the overhead wires to be installed, so instead of enlarging them, it was decided to build new tunnels running parallel to them, which took from 1949 until 1954. Electrification at 1,500 V dc was completed in 1955, but this technology was soon to become obsolete, as future wiring schemes would favour the 25 kV ac system.

In 1963 the British Railways Board was formed, with Dr Richard Beeching as its chairman. Within three months Beeching produced a highly controversial report entitled 'The Reshaping of British Railways'. This report, which famously came to be known as the 'Beeching Axe', recommended the closure of around a third of Britain's 18,000 mile network with the aim of reducing the enormous financial losses that the system was making. (At its peak the network boasted around 8,000 stations, almost all of which would have at least four or five staff each – even if they only saw two or three trains a day! – and it was strongly felt that the costs involved were simply not justified.) However, not all of the closures it recommended were actually implemented.

In particular, there was a lot of duplication of routes. Different lines between the same places had often been built by separate companies to compete with each other, whereas nowadays the Government would most likely have developed a structured plan for construction of a national rail network. Indeed, many lines and stations had arisen purely on a speculative basis, on the grounds that traffic might materialise because of their presence, and with hindsight should probably never have been built in the first place, since they were so unlikely to be a commercial success. Beeching felt that rationalising this would go a long way towards making the railways profitable, or at the very least, less of a financial burden. After all, with the country already virtually bankrupt from the Second World War, the Government could ill afford to keep on supporting a system that was making such huge losses. (At one point the railways employed as many as 700,000 people, which would be unsustainable with today's much higher labour costs.)

Because the process ended up being significantly more heavy-handed than was perhaps necessary in many cases, the mention of Beeching's name still provokes strong feelings of anger and resentment among many people – perhaps a little unfairly, since he did not himself have the power to actually close lines, only to recommend closures. (Interestingly, he refused to recommend closure of Manea Station in Cambridgeshire, due to 'the acute social hardship it would cause'.) Although he is likely to always be remembered as the 'Axeman', Beeching's primary aim was not, as is often made out, to destroy the railways, but to make them more sustainable. His report did also bring various benefits by eliminating hopelessly inefficient practices such as the use of loose-coupled freight trains, with small wagons whose brakes had to be released and applied individually. Containerisation and the introduction of continuous braking helped to make freight movements more efficient, while long distance electrification was another significant factor in modernising the railways. In fact, it could be argued that the real villain was possibly Ernest Marples, who was Minister of Transport at the time (and therefore did have the power to issue line closures), but also owned a large share of the road building company Marples & Ridgeway. This particular conflict of interest would never be permitted today for obvious reasons, and may explain the rashness of the actions taken.

Some time after the publication of Beeching's initial report, an even more drastic one was produced – 'The Development of the Major Railway Trunk Routes' – effectively suggesting that only around 3,000 miles of major intercity trunk routes should be selected for continued investment, and that all other lines should be closed. The main thinking behind this report was that there was still too much duplication in the network and that such overprovision was unjustified. (This is one possible sign of extreme heavy-handedness, because while there was a lot of unnecessary duplication, two or more lines running between the same points might also serve different intermediate places of similar importance. Also, one could prove a useful diversionary route for the other. Consequently, potentially eliminating duplication altogether was probably not necessary either.) This second report, which actually identified the Woodhead route as being worthy of remaining open, was rejected by the Government, and Beeching resigned in 1965.

However, the closure programme carried on until the early 1970s when it became apparent that, although the closures had achieved significant savings without which the network could easily have collapsed, they were not as high as had been hoped. It had been expected that, after closure of a line, people would drive to where the line had run to previously, before catching the train to their final destination. (The rise of the motor car had been one of the main reasons for the drop in rail passenger traffic.) However, it did not work out that way. Once people realised how much more convenient private motor cars were, they generally found it much easier to simply make their entire journey by road, with the result that some passengers were lost even from the surviving lines. This effect was possibly even more pronounced with freight traffic, due to the potentially time-consuming task of transferring goods from road to rail at the start of their journey and back to road at the other end.

As a result, the closures were virtually brought to a halt, though some did still occur from time to time. In particular, it was felt that two routes from Manchester to Sheffield could not be justified and passenger services were withdrawn from the Woodhead route in 1970. (By this time, the UK rail network had shrunk from around 18,000 miles and 7,000 stations to 12,000 miles and 2,500 stations – roughly the same size it is today.)

The line closed altogether in 1981 – a decision which many people still regard as being very short-sighted, as it meant the journey time from Manchester to Sheffield was increased from 35 minutes to around 75. There have been campaigns to reopen it, but so far these have not come to fruition. The section from Manchester to Hadfield and Glossop is still open to passengers, while at the

Sheffield end the line still exists as far as Stocksbridge; although the latter portion is no longer electrified. The two original single bores of tunnel at Woodhead have been used for carrying electric cables, and various plans have been proposed to use the third tunnel for this purpose as well. However, there has been strong opposition to any such proposal as it would put paid to any prospect of the line ever being reopened.

The Matlock to Buxton route was partially a product of the fierce competition between the two biggest rivals of the pre-grouping era – the London and North Western Railway and the Midland Railway. The latter opened a line from Ambergate to Rowsley in 1849, while the Stockport, Disley and Whaley Bridge Railway, which was owned by the LNWR, reached Buxton in 1863. This blocked the Midland's plans for a line to Manchester, but the company still extended their line from Rowsley to Buxton at about the same time.

In 1867, the Midland extended from Miller's Dale to New Mills and joined with the Manchester, Sheffield and Lincolnshire Railway's route into Manchester London Road, thereby giving the Midland a direct route from Manchester to London in addition to the LNWR's route, which is now the West Coast Main Line.

The Matlock to Buxton section closed in 1968, but in 1991 the Peak Railway Society reopened a short portion from Matlock to Darley Dale as a tourist line. This was extended in 1997 to a new station at Rowsley South, just outside Rowsley village. There have been numerous proposals considered to reopen the line to Buxton to help keep cars out of the Peak District National Park, but many doubts have been raised over the financial viability of such a scheme. However, the route of the line has been protected from development by Derbyshire County Council.

CHAPTER 2

THE START OF WORK

The long years of campaigning and fundraising were over, and the Peak Railway Society members were finally in a position to replace the bridge over the main road at Rowsley. This had been a major financial obstacle to the plans for rebuilding the line, but at last the money had been raised and work was ready to start. Sam Huncoat, the Station Master at Rowsley South, was becoming acquainted with the team of workers who would carry out the reopening work – both the replacement of the bridge and the rebuilding of the line beyond to Buxton.

"Good morning, gentlemen," he said cordially.

"Good morning, Mr Huncoat," replied Mark Failsworth, the team leader. "We're here to start work on the bridge."

"Yes, that's excellent. This is a very significant step for the railway – we've been wanting to reopen the line to Buxton for some time, but this has been one of the biggest barriers. It's great that you can now start!"

"Right, let's get to work!" called Mark to the team.

The men soon reached the site where the bridge was to cross the main road into Rowsley, and began to set up scaffolding as a means of a temporary 'bridge' from which to work. The road had been closed to allow the scaffolding to be erected, so that the work could be carried out unimpeded. Within two or three days the scaffolding was in place, with sheeting round it to screen off the wind, and the road was reopened to traffic, but with a temporary speed restriction in order to minimise vibration. This was vital to ensure that the task could be completed as safely as possible.

Meanwhile, the men who had been selected to carry out the reopening of the Woodhead route were assembled at Hadfield and poised to start work. David Waterfoot, the head of that team, was already examining the first half-mile of trackbed out of Hadfield and deciding how best to proceed with the plans. After this part was re-laid, the rest of the task would be fairly straightforward as it would involve laying the line across open countryside.

Back at Rowsley, the team members there were installing the main girders for the bridge. This was a very exacting operation, as they needed to be lowered into place with great care and precision. Liam Shankwell, one of the engineers on the team, was directing the crane lowering the first girder into position. Once it was positioned, Daniel Welshman (who, despite his name, had actually lived all his life in Glossop!) fixed the ends down. This process took several hours to complete, but everyone knew that it had to be done precisely; if the girders were not properly erected, the bridge would be very dangerous. By the end of the day, the girders had all been installed and the men were reflecting on their handiwork.

"We've done a pretty good job, I think," remarked Paul Handforth. "We should have this job finished in no time!"

"Well, it's gone alright so far," said Peter Mitchell. "But there's still a long way to go yet. For starters, we've got to put in the deck of the bridge – that's going to take a while. What's more, reinstalling this bridge is only part of the job; we've got about twenty miles of line to rebuild yet. I just hope nothing goes wrong."

"Oh, don't be so pessimistic!" remarked Paul in exasperation.

Elsewhere, the Woodhead team members had already relaid the line across to the other side of Hadfield and were now out on the open moor. While the men stopped for a tea break, Michael Portree was already admiring the view and appreciating what a difficult job it must have been to have built the line in the first place – thank goodness most of the heavy work had already been done for them! They sat down and began discussing the route and what its reopening would mean.

"You know, I really don't understand why they closed this line in the first place. I mean, even Beeching wanted to keep it open!"

"Yeah," agreed Dean Cartwright. "After all, for a major city, Sheffield isn't the easiest of places to get to from this side of the country – why close a fast electrified line into it? In fact, it's got to be one of the most important cities in the country without an electrified line!"

Adam Garsdale took a hearty swig from his mug before adding, "Exactly! It's a nightmare driving over that Snake Pass. Why they've never built a motorway between Manchester and Sheffield beats me!"

"Well, it might happen one of these days," remarked Neil Denting. "In the meantime, we're making sure there's at least one fast route between them! That's a pretty good start!"

"Hear, hear!" piped up the others.

"There was actually a plan to use the tunnel at Woodhead for a motorway once," put in Michael.

"Really?" replied Neil. "Well, the fact that they didn't go ahead with it has been a bit of a mixed blessing – on the one hand it means it's still a difficult journey by road, but on the other hand if it had been built, we wouldn't have been able to reopen this line!"

"Indeed," said Adam. "Funny how these things work out sometimes!"

Despite the associated extra cost, it had been decided to reopen the Woodhead route as an electrified line – as it had previously been – due to the desire to not merely provide an extra route from Manchester to Sheffield, but a faster one as well.

At Rowsley, however, extra costs were proving much more troublesome. Although the work on the bridge had now been completed, once again allowing trains to run into Rowsley itself, the cost had been much greater than anticipated. As a result, the original plan for a double track line had had to be scrapped and the men found that they would have to make do with a single track for the time being.

Peter Mitchell complained this was a sign that the scheme would fail, but the others were fairly confident it would be a one-off. After all, revising the plan would save much more money than the extra cost of rebuilding the bridge, so there might be some spare!

Chapter 3

TUNNEL TROUBLES

Some time after the work on the bridge at Rowsley was completed, Mark Failsworth's team started inspecting the old tunnel at Haddon. Although the trackbed had been used as a walking route for some years, the tunnel had been blocked off by huge metal gates at each end. These had now been removed to allow the men to gain access. They tramped down it, sporting orange hi-visibility vests, blue jeans and white hard hats with lamps attached to them, carefully examining the tunnel roof. It was very important to make sure that this was safe before any trains ran through – the last thing they would want would be for the roof to collapse on top of one!

The men had penetrated some way into the tunnel when Liam Shankwell noticed a sizeable crack in the roof. Making a note of its position, he then looked at the trundle wheel that Mark had been wheeling along to measure the distance from the tunnel mouth by which they had entered, and noted that as well.

Almost as soon as he finished taking notes, Liam noticed the crack starting to grow larger. He didn't like the look of it one bit and shouted to the others:

"We've got to get out of here!"

The men immediately turned and started to run back the way they had come. Most of them managed to turn tail just in time before that part of the roof caved in, completely blocking the tunnel. However, Peter had been a bit slow on the uptake, and was not so lucky.

"Pete, are you alright?" Liam called through the debris, after realising that he was not with them.

"Yeah, I'm fine," came the reply. "I'm not hurt. Nothing's fallen on me, but I'm cut off from you all!"

"Thank goodness for that! No problem. You can just walk down to the other end of the tunnel, then walk across the top to rejoin us."

"That's a good idea. See you in a bit."

Peter didn't fancy the idea of climbing over the steep hills to rejoin the rest of the team, but nevertheless he felt he was lucky to be alive. Trying to be positive, he began to walk away from the blockage towards the north end of the tunnel. He had almost reached it when, suddenly, a second collapse occurred right in front of him! Now he was trapped! Panicking, he ran back to the first pile of debris and called desperately:

"Liam, are you still there?"

"Yeah, I'm still here." he replied, somewhat surprised by Peter's continued presence.

Peter was relieved. His worst fear had been that the men would have walked away to wait for him outside!

"You'll never guess what's happened!"

"Don't tell me – there's been another collapse!"

"Correct!"

"Oh, marvellous! Anyway, don't worry – we'll send a message to the Mountain Rescue. In the meantime, we'll have to try and shift some of this rock so that you can get out."

It took several hours to clear the debris from the two blockages and allow Peter to escape from the tunnel, after which it was decided that extra work should be carried out to make it safe. Temporary steel braces were installed to support the roof while it was inspected and strengthened, the added cost of which made the men thankful that they had decided to proceed with a single track line despite originally budgeting for double track.

Meanwhile, the Woodhead team had experienced no such problems. As a new tunnel had been built when the line was electrified, the Woodhead tunnel was much newer and found to be structurally sound. As a result, the go-ahead was given for the reinstallation of the overhead wires inside the tunnel, and David Waterfoot was overseeing this process while Adam Garsdale made sure the roof gantries were secure. The relaying of the five miles of track between Hadfield and Woodhead had proceeded at a phenomenal rate, despite the additional job of installing overhead line equipment, and confidence among the team was high.

The problems with Haddon Tunnel, however, had done very little for the team's confidence there. Just as they were about to enter the tunnel to prepare it for the relaying of track, Peter called out, "I don't want to go in that tunnel! What if it falls down again?"

"Don't be such a coward," answered Mark. "It's quite safe – we've repaired it now."

"Strood Tunnel once collapsed after it had been repaired," said Peter, clearly unconvinced.

"Yes, but the second collapse was at a different point to where it had been repaired. No chance of that here – we've relined the whole tunnel! Anyway, Strood used to be a canal tunnel so it's much older than a lot of railway tunnels and so more likely to collapse, now come on!"

Still nervous, Peter reluctantly joined the rest of the men and entered the tunnel.

Chapter 4

SNOW PROBLEMS

The Pennines can be an extremely inhospitable place during the winter, and being trapped on a mountain in a severe snowstorm is undoubtedly a hazardous situation to be in. The chance of getting lost is increased significantly, visibility can be very poor in heavy snowfall, and the dangers of contracting frostbite or hypothermia are much too unpleasant to describe.

Despite all this, the Matlock team continued working on Haddon Tunnel during the winter. With the cost of rebuilding having already risen significantly, they were anxious to not lose any more time in construction and so toiled on regardless. The cold wind blew through the tunnel, making the men shiver and their teeth chatter while they laid the new track. Despite the original plan for a double track line having had to be scrapped, the track was laid to one side of the tunnel rather than in the middle, the anticipation being that one day double track might eventually be reinstated.

On one occasion, the men had foolishly forgotten to check the weather forecast and set off into the tunnel, completely unaware that an extremely heavy snowfall was on the way. All day long they worked hard, oblivious to the fact that snow was falling heavily outside. As it became more and more intense, the men agreed it would not be a good idea to try to leave during the snowfall, so they decided to shelter in the tunnel until the snow stopped falling. They sat down with their backs to the wall, waiting for the weather to improve.

After several hours, however, it became apparent that the snow was not showing any sign of stopping soon and the men became restless. Suddenly, an avalanche occurred, blocking the north end of the tunnel and making it more difficult for the men to get out. Peter was terrified; it reminded him of the roof collapses and he hoped they wouldn't be trapped.

"I hate tunnels!" he muttered to himself.

"Don't go on, Pete," said Liam, happening to overhear him. "We're all in the same boat now."

"That makes it worse. If we *all* get stuck here, how can we get anyone to help? You can't get a mobile phone signal in a tunnel!"

"We'll think of something."

Hours later still, the snow had built up round the south end of the tunnel and the men realised that if they didn't act soon, they would indeed be trapped. They picked up shovels and began to dig through the snow. It was a tiring job, not to mention frustrating; as soon as they shifted the snow, more seemed to fall into the place where it had been. Eventually they managed to make a clearing to allow Paul Handforth and Liam to leave the tunnel and fetch help, while the others stayed behind and huddled close together for warmth.

About half an hour later, a snow plough came chugging down the track towards the tunnel, clearing the trackbed along the way. The men were rescued and, after a short discussion, it was reluctantly decided to suspend work on the line until the weather improved.

The Woodhead team, on the other hand, had been much more sensible with regards to the weather. Anticipating that there would most likely be snow, they had erected temporary snow sheds at either end of the Woodhead tunnel to prevent them from being trapped by avalanches. The work inside the tunnel consequently proceeded unhindered, despite the fact that it was still cold and draughty. Furthermore, the team always made sure to check the weather forecasts before setting off to the site each day. When they heard that there was going to be a particularly heavy snowfall, they sensibly decided not to proceed with work that day. In addition, once they realised there was no sign of it improving any time soon, they took the decision to suspend work. Being already significantly ahead of schedule, they could well afford to.

CHAPTER 5

FROM BAD TO WORSE

The fortunes of the Matlock-Buxton team didn't improve once the snow disappeared. Some time later, the men were inspecting the viaduct at Miller's Dale, which needed a lot of work on it before it could carry trains again. The laying of track from Haddon Tunnel had proved to be a tricky operation; freeze-thaw damage to the trackbed, caused by the snow, had had to be repaired. As a result, the track was still several miles from the viaduct, but it had been decided to carry out an advance inspection of it anyway due to the amount of work that would be needed.

"Nothing seems to be going right," Peter had said when the freeze-thaw damage had been discovered. "I'm beginning to wonder if this reopening might have been a bit too ambitious."

"Pete, you worry too much," Liam had replied. "We're away from the tunnel now, so what more could go wrong?"

Peter had flatly refused to work in the tunnel after they had nearly been trapped by the snow. Instead, he had been given the job of making sure there had been no damage to the track that had already been laid between the tunnel and Rowsley. Thankfully, this section had survived the cold weather, but the damage to the rest of the trackbed had significantly cut into the budget, and the cost overruns were now threatening to wipe out the saving achieved by deciding on a single track line.

Some months later, the tracklaying finally reached the viaduct and work on it began. Heavy scaffolding was erected to hold up the structure while the weak spots were identified. Once the pillars had been strengthened, the heavy scaffolding was removed while lighter scaffolding was erected, merely to provide a platform to work on. Learning their lesson from the incident at Haddon Tunnel, the team suspended work during the winter, though thankfully this winter was not as bad as the previous one and consequently there was little or no freeze-thaw damage to contend with.

One day, when the sun was shining brightly, the men were assembled on the deck of the viaduct, having completed the strengthening work and tracklaying on it.

"Well, things finally seem to be looking up!" said Daniel Welshman.

"Yes, indeed!" agreed Liam. "At this rate, we should reach Buxton in no time!"

Barely were the words out of his mouth than he noticed the scaffolding was creaking. It began to rock and sway dangerously in the high winds, while the men watched helplessly. Then, to their horror, the scaffolding collapsed with an almighty crash. The men were dumbstruck.

"You and your big mouth!" snorted Peter at Liam.

"Dear, dear," said Mark in shock. "Thank goodness we weren't on the scaffolding – that could've been very nasty indeed!"

"Yeah, thank goodness," agreed Paul.

That proved to be the only consolation for the team: they were given a hefty fine for breach of Health and Safety regulations, leaving them with virtually no margin for error with regards to the budget. Peter became more pessimistic than ever about the project being successful, while even some of the others had to admit that the situation was now looking increasingly grave.

As if that wasn't enough, some time later a serious landslide occurred in a cutting just beyond the viaduct while the men were working on relaying track through it. Most of them managed to escape in time, but Paul wasn't so lucky: as he was struggling to catch up with the others, a falling tree landed on top of him, leaving his left leg so badly crushed that it had to be amputated below the knee. This led to a compensation claim, as he could no longer work. The case was won, which left the team in a very desperate situation indeed.

CHAPTER 6

A DESPERATE APPEAL

Paul's compensation claim, coupled with the cost of repairing the landslide, had left the team in a very difficult situation. There was now not enough money left in the budget to complete the line, so they realised that they would have to apply for extra funding to cover the additional costs.

"I'm not sure they'll agree, but we've got to try," Mark told the others, when they met to decide what to do.

"Let's forget it," said Peter miserably. "This whole idea was doomed from the start – it's just not meant to happen."

"Don't be like that," replied Liam. "I know the Government were reluctant to fund the reopening of this line in the first place, but we managed to persuade them."

"They're probably thinking that they were right to have doubts over it, and I can't say I blame them."

"We'll have to meet with them and see if we can persuade them."

"You lot can go – I won't bother. It'll be a waste of time."

A few days later, the team met at Manchester Piccadilly to catch the train to London. After much persuasion, Peter had reluctantly agreed to travel with them, despite his continued feeling that their meeting with the Government would be a waste of time.

The Pendolino stopped at Stockport and Stoke-on-Trent before continuing on the rest of its journey, scheduled to be non-stop to London. It raced through the Trent Valley, gliding along smoothly and gracefully. However, just after passing through Atherstone, it began to lose speed quite significantly.

"Why are we slowing down? We're not supposed to be stopping at Nuneaton," said Liam.

"Maybe it's just a signal check," replied Mark. "We should pick up again in a bit."

But they didn't. As they approached Nuneaton, the train became slower and slower until it came to a complete halt at the station – it had slowed so much that it had only just managed to stop with all the carriages next to the platform. Minutes later, a member of the train crew walked down the aisle of the carriage informing the passengers that the train had broken down and that they would have to catch another one to London.

"Brilliant!" said Peter. "Just marvellous! Now we're going to be late. I told you it was a waste of time!"

"Come on, Pete," said Liam reassuringly. "At least this time it isn't our fault."

"Like that makes any difference. We're still not going to be on time!"

"Well, at least we can watch the trains go by," said Daniel, trying to put a positive light on the situation.

The men sat down on seats to wait for another train. At that point there was a two-tone horn blast from the direction of London, and seconds later another Pendolino shot through the station on its way to Glasgow.

"See?" Daniel added. "You don't really notice their speed when you're travelling on them – it's only when you see them go past now that you can appreciate it."

"A fat lot of good that is if they break down!" snorted Peter.

No-one responded this time. Growing increasingly tired of Peter's sceptical attitude, the others decided it was pointless trying to convince him, and realised it was probably better to hope for the best in the meeting. A Class 50 'Thunderbird' locomotive was summoned to drag the failed train away, and the men watched it chug out of the station in the direction of Birmingham. They became increasingly bored with waiting, and were grateful when, after what seemed like ages, the tannoy crackled into life:

"The train arriving on Platform 5 is the 09:41 London Midland service to London Euston – calling at Rugby, Long Buckby, Northampton, Wolverton, Milton Keynes Central, Bletchley, Leighton Buzzard, Cheddington, Tring, Berkhamstead, Hemel Hempstead, Apsley, King's Langley, Watford Junction and London Euston."

"That's going to take ages with all those stops!" moaned Peter.

"Just get on the thing!" snapped Mark, as a Class 350 Desiro drew up at the platform. "Better late than never!"

The team boarded the train, which did indeed take some time to reach London, and they eventually disembarked at Euston Station before proceeding to the underground taxi rank to take a couple of cabs to the Houses of Parliament. Although he would never admit it to Peter, Mark was starting to wonder if their project was a bit ambitious. However, he kept his thoughts to himself and began to concentrate on the forthcoming meeting. Would they be able to get the emergency funding, or would the Government also think the project was more trouble than it was worth?

CHAPTER 7

RAPID PROGRESS

The situation on the Woodhead route, on the other hand, had been significantly different. Whereas the Matlock team's progress had been seriously hampered by various problems, the Woodhead team had been racing across the Pennines at a rate of knots. The stringing of overhead wires inside the three-and-a-half miles of Woodhead Tunnel had been a time-consuming process, but once this was completed, the work had been proceeding at a steady but rapid pace. The team members were exceptionally pleased with themselves; they felt they had worked very hard on the project, so they proceeded relentlessly.

"Well done, team," said David Waterfoot, when he addressed them one day. "At the rate we're going, we could have this line finished by the end of the year!"

The process of tracklaying was a lot quicker than when the line had been built in the first place: originally the sleepers would have been laid individually with the rails being fixed to them one by one, but the modern process was much simpler. There were flat beds carrying sections of track with the rails already fixed to the sleepers with chairs, plus equipment on moving gantries to lower these prefabricated sections onto the trackbed before being joined together, thus allowing much greater accuracy with positioning. The rails were also welded into longer lengths instead of being joined together by bolted fishplates, thus providing a smoother ride for the passengers.

Even continuously welded rails are subject to expansion and

contraction, so gaps of a few millimetres still have to be left in the rails occasionally to allow room for the process. However, instead of the rail ends being blunt, as they are with track laid the more traditional way, these are tapered so that the train wheels pass over them at an angle rather than 'bumping' straight across. This makes journeys much smoother. Welded rails tend to be used on most long distance routes, but some commuter and rural branch lines still use bolted rail joints with expansion gaps between each of them, which causes the 'clickety-clack' sound that the trains make on the track.

Another process that was able to proceed much quicker than the previous time was the electrification of the route. Previously, the overhead line masts had had to be erected and assembled one by one next to the track, but the use of mobile electrification 'work-shops' had also speeded up this process. These vehicles consisted of flat beds on which pre-assembled masts were laid, with moving arms attached to the sides. These arms gripped the masts and turned them upright before lowering them into their foundations, where they were then fixed down.

Behind the flat beds were enormous wooden drums with copper cables wound round them. These were unwound as the work proceeded further along the line, while the workers attached them to the insulators suspended from the masts. It was crucial to fix the cables at precisely the right tension, because if they were too slack, any expansion in warm weather could cause them to droop too low over the tracks. On the other hand, if they were too tight then contraction in cold weather could cause them to pull at the masts and possibly snap. Furthermore, the wires do not run exactly parallel to the rails, but in a slight zig-zag manner. The purpose of this is to spread wear on the trains' pantographs, as otherwise the friction would eventually slice them in two – most undesirable!

All these processes allowed the route to be laid much quicker than it ever would have been if older methods had been used. As a result, within a few months of starting work on it, the team had reached Stocksbridge.

"This is excellent!" remarked David when this happened. "We need to inspect the existing track between here and Sheffield to see what condition it's in and whether we need to replace it, but otherwise we've effectively done the hard part. All that'll remain after this is to re-electrify this bit!"

"And put in a new chord in Sheffield," added Michael Portree.

"Yes, of course. It needs to run into the existing station now that Victoria is closed."

"Still, it's quite exciting that we've already got this far," said Dean Cartwright.

The inspection of the Stocksbridge to Sheffield portion was carried out over the following weeks, and some track was found to be overgrown and in need of replacement. However, the vegetation clearance and relaying were soon dealt with and the team then continued to proceed with the electrification and the restoration of stations along the route.

"They must've spelt this station name wrongly," Adam Garsdale pointed out one day when they were working on one of the stations.

"What do you mean?" asked Neil Denting.

"It says 'Oughty Bridge', but the village is called Oughtibridge. Why the difference?"

"No idea. It's just one of those peculiarities – they've always been spelt differently. I wouldn't worry about it, Adam. As long as they can get on and off trains here, I don't think most people mind how it's spelt!"

Adam turned back to the process of resurfacing the platform while Neil continued to remove weeds from the stonework.

The restoration of Oughty Bridge Station – along with the other stations on the Stocksbridge-Sheffield section – was a painstaking task, and one that the men were determined to complete to a very high standard. Over the following weeks they toiled relentlessly, buoyed by the fact that this was the final section of the line and it wouldn't be long before it could be reopened. The new chord was installed to allow trains to run from the Woodhead route into the

formerly named Sheffield Pond Street (and later Midland) Station –
now simply called Sheffield – and the overhead wires were erected
along the line to once again make it possible to run electric trains
across the Pennines.

Eventually, the time came for the grand reopening. The work
had taken barely a year to complete, and the team members were
extremely proud of themselves as they assembled at Sheffield
Station, watching a Desiro unit arrive from Manchester – the first
electric train to run into Sheffield under its own power for over 30
years!

"Look at that, boys!" called David. "That's all because of us,
that is!"

"You know, if this doesn't strengthen the case for electrifying
the Midland Main Line, then nothing will!" remarked Michael.

"Indeed!" agreed Adam.

After this, the line continued to thrive. Many people who hated
the precarious drive over the Snake Pass from Manchester to
Sheffield were now perfectly happy to take the train instead, given
that the journey could now be completed in less than half the time
it took travelling via the Hope Valley route. Overall, the scheme
was generally perceived as a success and showed just what could
be done.

CHAPTER 8

THE LAST CHANCE SALOON

It had taken a lot of persuasion, but finally the Government had been convinced to allow the Matlock team an emergency grant to cover the cost overruns. Citing the success of the Woodhead route, which by then had already been open for some months, the men had put together a very strong and convincing case for continuing with their scheme. However, the Government were still not happy about all the problems that had so far occurred, and had only agreed to hand over the additional funding on condition that nothing further went wrong. Any further cost increases and the team would have to find funding from elsewhere – a prospect which the men found really daunting, but they were determined to make sure that there were no further mishaps.

They were all assembled at Miller's Dale ready to resume work, while Mark Failsworth explained all this to them:

"…and so we need to be extra vigilant. Nothing must go wrong, because I can't imagine it being particularly easy to find any more funding from elsewhere. Basically, any more mishaps and that's the end for this project! Right, let's get back to work!"

The workers proceeded to the end of the line and began to lay new track – Mark's dire warnings still ringing in their ears. Peter continued to be sceptical about the success and was sure something else would indeed go wrong, but by now he had learned to keep these feelings to himself while he and the team worked. Finally, at the end of the day, they reflected on their progress.

"Well, we've done brilliantly today," Liam said brightly. "Let's hope this is how we mean to carry on."

"Yeah. We really can't afford any more slip-ups," agreed Daniel.

The next day's work also proceeded without any problems, and so did the day after that. Although the men were under immense pressure to complete the work without incident, they seemed to thrive on it and were working harder than ever. However, none of them dared say anything about how well they felt the line was proceeding, for fear of tempting fate!

Over the next two or three months they continued to progress with extra vigilance, determined to make a success of the job. Even Peter was starting to feel that they might pull it off, but he wisely kept his thoughts to himself as he didn't want to put a jinx on it!

Eventually, the team found that the line was nearing completion, and the sight of Buxton on the horizon was extremely welcome! After relaying the track as far as the nearby quarry, the time had finally come for the last section of track to be laid, connecting the new line to the existing one from Buxton. The team fixed the rails into place with a feeling of intense satisfaction and – in some cases – relief!

"Well, we've done it!" exclaimed Daniel.

"Finally!" shouted Liam.

"At last!" sighed Peter.

"Yes, we've all done an excellent job," added Mark. "It's great that we've managed to get the line reconnected. Now we need to arrange test runs."

After this, numerous test runs were made on the new line. The team still had to be vigilant, as the last thing anyone wanted was for the construction to be completed without any further mishaps only for something to go wrong with the trains on the line! At long last, the tests were completed and the line was given the all-clear to reopen to passengers – 18 months behind schedule.

Chapter 9

THE ACID TEST

The special train, comprising a gleaming rake of bright red LMS coaches, stood below the impressive, lofty trainshed roof at London St Pancras Station. It was to have the privilege of becoming the first passenger-carrying train to run over the reopened line from Matlock to Buxton, thus following the Midland Railway's original main route from London to Manchester. One man stood next to the front of the train, talking to another that he had just met.

"Great to meet you. We've come up from Tenterden."

"Oh, by the Kent and East Sussex Railway?" asked the second.

"Yeah. I tell you what, getting here is so much easier since they built the high speed line. Previously it used to take a long time coming by train from Ashford – I mean, no-one in their right mind brings a car into Central London these days if they can possibly avoid it!"

"Indeed not!"

"Anyway, we drove to Ashford and then got the high speed service here – previously we would've gone into Victoria on the classic route, so we would've had the added hassle of getting across to here, whereas the new route brings us directly into St Pancras!"

"That's handy!"

"Yeah. I must say, they've done a fabulous job with this station; it's an excellent departure point for Eurostars. Sorry, what's your name?"

"Graham Axminster."

"I'm Eddie. Eddie Piper. This should be a great trip!"

"Yeah, I'm really looking forward to it!"

"It's a pity about the traction, though. I mean, if they have to have a diesel at the start at all, they might at least have had something a bit more nostalgic!"

Both men turned to look at the Class 67 locomotive at the head of the train.

"Yeah," agreed Graham. "Still, at least we'll get the real stuff on when we get to Matlock!"

After a while, Eddie was sitting at a table in a First Class carriage with his wife and their two children while they waited for the train to leave. Eventually, a whistle was heard from the platform and the train began to chug out of the station, passing a Class 222 Meridian unit as it did so.

The train proceeded at a moderate pace as it negotiated the Midland Main Line through the London suburbs, travelling under the wires of the Thameslink system. It made intermediate stops at St Albans, Luton and Bedford to pick up passengers, after which it left the wires behind and proceeded to the next pick-up point at Kettering. At this point, Eddie and his son left the train to look at the locomotive.

"Where does that line go?" asked the boy, indicating the line branching off to the right in the distance.

"That's the line to Corby – it's not long been reopened to passengers. Until then, Corby was the largest town in Europe without a station!"

"Blimey!"

"Yes, Simon. Remarkable, isn't it?"

A few minutes later, Eddie and Simon returned to their coach and sat down at their table again. Simon turned to his sister and started explaining what their father had told him about the line to Corby.

"It seems Corby Station has actually been reopened twice!"

"Really?" asked his sister excitedly.

"Yes, Helen. Quite remarkable!"

"I'll say!"

As the train began to move out of the station, the children became more and more excited. They watched the Corby branch disappear off to the opposite side of the train, while it proceeded further north on its journey. After additional intermediate stops at Leicester and Loughborough, the train left the Midland Main Line to take the line to Derby, where it made one final pick-up. It then carried on towards Ambergate, where it deviated from the main route and started along the single line towards Matlock.

As the train pulled into Matlock Station, some of the staff from the Peak Railway Society were assembled to greet it. Many of the passengers stepped out onto the platform to watch the locomotive being uncoupled from the coaches before it was swapped. The Pipers stood by the front of the train as the diesel chugged away into a siding, and Eddie turned to Simon and said, "Well, son – now we get the proper stuff on!"

Simon watched intently as an LMS Black 5 steam locomotive slowly reversed alongside the platform and gently buffered up to the coaches. A man in an orange hi-visibility vest jumped down in between the tender of the locomotive and the coaches and began to unhook black hoses from the ends of each of the vehicles, before screwing them together.

"What are those for?" asked Simon.

"They're for the brakes," replied Eddie. "Those chains that they connect to the hooks keep the coaches coupled to the loco, but they have to be able to stop them as well! It's thought that failure to connect the hoses caused a very nasty accident at Grantham in 1906."

A loud hiss issued from the brake hoses after they were connected; Eddie explained that they were testing the hoses were properly fixed and there were no leaks – after all, they wouldn't want a repeat of the Grantham accident! Simon enjoyed watching the men at work, and Helen was pleased to see her brother so happy.

They returned to their seats, and a loud blast from the whistle was heard before the train gradually began to puff out of the station, swapping Network Rail metals for those of the Peak Railway Society. The scenery that the line travelled through was very spectacular and the family thoroughly enjoyed it.

"We're not going very fast, are we?" Simon pointed out, sometime after they had left Rowsley behind.

"Well, that's because it's all uphill to Buxton – it's the highest town in England!" Eddie replied. "Anyway, look at that scenery. You wouldn't want it to go too fast or you wouldn't be able to admire it!"

"Certainly not!" added his wife.

"No, Louise. Walking through it is fine, but it's very tiring! At least this way, you can see it in comfort!"

Despite the reopening of the line having deprived walkers of one possible way of seeing the scenery, many had still managed to find excellent vantage points from which to watch the train travel by. A large group of them stood together at the top of a mountain peak near Haddon Tunnel, watching the train steam along the bottom of the cutting.

"It's like a great red serpent slithering along!" remarked one young boy, as the train snaked its way round the hills.

"A fire-breathing one at that!" added his sister, as it gave a couple of blasts on its whistle before plunging into the tunnel and out of sight.

Meanwhile, in the Premier Dining Class coaches, the team who had rebuilt the line to Buxton sat in anticipation as the train traversed the route. They had travelled to London the night before in order to be on the train at the start. Naturally, they had been very nervous about this part of the journey; with all the problems that had already occurred with the construction, they could ill afford anything to go wrong this time!

"I hope this tunnel doesn't collapse again!" said Peter nervously, as they entered it.

"You worry too much, Pete – just enjoy the ride!" retorted Liam, even though he was secretly a bit apprehensive himself.

Mark ignored them and carried on reading his newspaper. He was extremely confident that nothing would go wrong, as they had made every effort to ensure the route was safe when the conditions for the additional grant had been laid down.

Sure enough, the train emerged from the tunnel completely unscathed and Peter noticeably breathed a sigh of relief. Eventually, it steamed onto the line from Buxton to Manchester, leaving behind the newly-built route and ensuring that there was nothing more for the team to worry about. After all, the return journey was to be via the Woodhead route, which had already been open for some months.

Thirsty from the climb, the train stopped at Stockport to take on water. Once more the Pipers left their carriage and walked along the platform to watch this fascinating process.

"Be careful not to trip over the hoses," warned Eddie. "They have to top it up every 70 miles or so – more frequently if it's been going uphill a lot, like it has now."

"Where do they get the water from?" asked Simon. "There doesn't seem to be a water tower here."

"There's a tanker parked on the road outside the station – they run hoses from it into the tender."

While the locomotive took on water, the engine crew invited children into the cab for a few minutes at a time. Simon jumped at the chance and was even allowed to sit in the driver's seat.

"I'm James Stevenson," said the driver. "What's your name?"

"Simon Piper."

"Pleased to meet you," said the fireman. "I'm Chris Chapelton."

"What does that big red lever do?" asked Simon.

"That's the regulator – it controls how fast the train goes," explained James. "It's like the accelerator in a car; it varies the amount of steam that goes into the cylinders, just as a car accelerator controls how much fuel goes into the engine."

"Oh. What's that big wheel with the handle for?"

"That's the reverser. It works like gears. When we start off, we turn it fully forward or backward to give us as much pulling power as possible. That uses a lot of steam though, which is why we have to wind it down as we speed up – just like changing up the gears in a car."

"Ah, right."

"Yeah. In a car you use a low gear when you need more power, like when you're going uphill. It's the same with this. When we go uphill, we wind the reverser up."

Simon was intrigued by the workings of the locomotive, and the driver and fireman continued to explain all sorts of other controls and gauges. They mentioned that there were two steam pressure gauges – one showing the pressure in the boiler, and the other the pressure in the cylinders, the latter being known as the steam chest pressure. At the moment, this was at zero because the train was stopped and the regulator was closed. There were also two very small wheels, which the fireman explained were the injectors that moved water from the tender into the boiler, using steam to do so. One, the live steam valve, used steam straight from the boiler; while the other, the exhaust steam valve, used steam from the cylinders – although the latter could not really be used while the train was stationary, as there was no steam in the cylinders.

"What's this lever down here for?"

"That controls the cylinder cocks; they're openings in the cylin-ders," James said. "When the train has stopped, the steam can build up in the cylinders and condense into water, so we have to open them to allow it to drain out. That's why you'll see steam coming out of the cylinders when the train starts moving."

"I see."

"We have to make sure we close them at that point though, otherwise the steam gets wasted and it's harder to move the train!"

Simon chuckled.

"That would never do!"

"Indeed not! Anyway, we'll be due to leave soon, so you'd better get back. Mind you don't fall over the coals."

Simon stepped carefully over the loose lumps of coal scattered over the cab floor, before climbing down onto the platform and rejoining his family to get back on the train. It steamed out of the station to cheers and waves from many people on the platform and continued northwards.

Instead of traversing the main line into Manchester, the train deviated onto the little-used line towards Stalybridge. At this point, Eddie said to his children, "Yes, this is an interesting bit. This line normally only has one train a week – and it only runs one way!"

"What's the point of that?" asked Helen, puzzled.

"Well, to close the line would need an Act of Parliament, and in this case they reckon it's easier and cheaper to simply run the minimum service required to keep it open – i.e. one train a week in one direction. Such a train is known as a 'Parliamentary', or 'Parly' for short."

"Do people actually use it, Dad?" asked Simon.

"Oh, yes! When it runs, they all pile onto it so that no-one can complain it isn't being used! That way the line stays open!"

Simon chuckled.

"If it only runs one way, how do they get back?"

"Well, in this case they go into Manchester and out again. One thing they used to go in for was 'closure by stealth' – mostly by deliberately running trains at inconvenient times so that hardly anyone will use them, making it easier to make out a case for closing a line or station. Except it doesn't really work these days – people have got wise to it and have a habit of finding out when the trains are running and making sure that there are people on them!"

The train continued along the line, passing through the two intermediate stations at Reddish South and Denton before reaching the junction just north of the latter. There, instead of taking the right-hand line towards Stalybridge, it took the left-hand one which would join the line into Manchester Victoria. It continued to follow this route before rounding the chord at Miles Platting to take the line towards Rochdale. The train passed the junction for the closed line through Oldham, which was in the process of being converted for an extension of the Manchester Metrolink tram system.

Just south of Castleton, the train left the Rochdale line to join the rails of the East Lancashire Railway. It felt right at home on the line as it steamed through Bury Bolton Street and Ramsbottom, before finally reaching the end of its journey at Rawtenstall. The passengers all disembarked from the train and proceeded towards the exit, intent on finding something to do in the town before rejoining the train for their return journey. Simon watched as the locomotive was uncoupled from the train and began to run round it – a sight which he found particularly spectacular. Living in Tenterden, he had seen steam locomotives before on the Kent and East Sussex Railway, but they were all small light ones. This was a much bigger and more impressive machine!

CHAPTER 10

HOMEWARD BOUND

After spending a couple of hours exploring Rawtenstall, the passengers returned to the station. Simon was talking to the Station Master.

"Where did the engine turn round? I don't see a turntable."

"Well, it would've gone back down the line to Castleton. The lines there form a triangle, so it can go into those and turn round there. They'll also have refilled it with water and coal."

At that point, the rest of the Pipers arrived.

"Oh, hello there," said the Station Master. "I'm Joe Clacton. Your boy certainly seems very interested in trains, I must say!"

"Yes," replied Louise. "We live in Tenterden – it's at the end of the Kent and East Sussex Railway, so we often see the steam trains there."

"Ah, I see. Well, I trust you've had a great day!"

"Indeed we have!" said Eddie. "Well, see you again soon, I hope!"

They climbed back into the train and sat down at their seats. Some minutes later, the train began to pull out of the station, travelling back the way it had come. It rejoined the Rochdale line at Castleton and travelled towards Manchester before once again traversing the Miles Platting curve, then taking the short line to Ashburys where it connected with the route from Piccadilly. The train continued through Gorton, Fairfield and Hyde before making a stop at Hadfield to take on water.

"Again?" asked Simon in disbelief, when his father explained why they had stopped there.

"Well, there's another long climb ahead of us, so they want to make sure there's enough water to do it! It's quite a thirsty beast, this thing!"

After refilling with water, the train puffed out of Hadfield Station and onto the Woodhead route. Simon had been particularly looking forward to this bit as his father had already told him all about the route's closure and how it had been one line that many people had wanted to see reopened. Wishing to get a proper view of a steam locomotive in action, he walked to one of the vestibules and leaned out of the window. This enabled him to really experience the sights, sounds and smells of the train powering up the steep gradient to Woodhead. He was entranced by the sound of the pistons working very hard and the spectacular sight of the locomotive pulling the train, a thick plume billowing behind it from the chimney. Pointing this out, his father said, "See, when you look at that you can understand why it needs so much water!"

Meanwhile, the teams that had rebuilt the Matlock and Woodhead routes were being served dinner in Premier Class. After leaving the Matlock portion of the journey behind, the team had begun to relax and enjoy the day. By now the worries of anything possibly going wrong seemed a distant memory as they tucked into their food.

"Let's hope this tunnel doesn't collapse, eh, Pete?" joked Liam as they entered Woodhead Tunnel.

"Oh, shut up!" snapped Peter, and continued to concentrate on cutting his chicken.

The men continued to admire the view as the train travelled over the Pennines towards Sheffield. Once there, the steam locomotive was uncoupled and the Class 67, which had hauled the train on the outward journey as far as Matlock, was attached at the opposite end, having travelled up to Sheffield in the meantime. The train then chugged out of the station and travelled onto the line towards Worksop, before taking the Robin Hood Line through Mansfield to Nottingham.

"This line is proof that re-openings can be successful," remarked

Adam Garsdale to the other Woodhead team members. "Until it reopened, Mansfield was the largest town in Britain without a rail link."

"Blimey," said Dean Cartwright.

The two teams had been talking to each other about the contrasting fortunes of their reopening schemes, and had found the stories intriguing. The Matlock team felt pleased that the Woodhead team had faced hardly any problems and wished that their progress could have been as smooth, while the Woodhead team found the tales of the Matlock misfortunes amusing to some extent, but at the same time knew better than to show it.

The sight of the sunset as they travelled towards Nottingham was another highlight of the trip, and eventually the train stopped there to set down the passengers who had boarded at Derby on the outward journey. The Matlock team also left the train there, after many goodbyes and hearty exchanges with their Woodhead counterparts. They watched the train chug out of the station and waved to each other as they passed, before sitting down on seats to wait for the train back to Matlock.

Within a few minutes, a Class 158 unit drew up at the platform and the team climbed on and sat down at a table.

"This train seems a bit boring after the other one," said Liam. "Back to reality, eh?"

The others chuckled.

"Yeah," agreed Mark. "It is quite a climb-down!"

"Well, it's been quite a day!" remarked Daniel. "I must say I'm relieved nothing went wrong!"

"Me too!" agreed Peter. "If anything had gone wrong, it could've been a disaster. Still, I'm pleased that we managed it – eventually!"

"Hear, hear!" chorused the others.

They settled down to enjoy the journey back to Matlock and reflect on the day's events. It had been a long, hard effort, and there had been many problems along the way, but eventually they had achieved their goal. They realised that if you try hard enough, you will eventually succeed – and they were now confident that, having come through this first journey, the reopening would indeed prove to be a success.

The End

THE JINXED RAILWAY

After several years of campaigning, the Allingford and Winterbury Junction Railway have finally been granted an extension for their line to the seaside town of Dillingpool-on-Sea. Local landowner Thomas Harwood has been very reluctant to sell his land to allow the company to build the line, but eventually agrees after travelling by train to a meeting. When he travels on the first train, he is very impressed.

However, although the opening goes ahead without a hitch, the line is plagued with problems right from the start. This causes many people to begin to lose faith in the line, none more so than Harwood.

At first he is merely critical, but when a serious accident occurs involving his son Jack, he decides he has had enough and wants the line closed down. However, young Jack has maintained a strong belief in the line ever since its opening – not to mention a burning desire to become an engine driver. Will this be enough to save the line?

CHAPTER 1

AUTHORISATION

"I will not allow it!" shouted the farmer. "I absolutely will not allow it!"

"Oh, dry up, Thomas!" retorted the director. "I'm sure you'll change your mind once you see how great it is!"

"Humph!"

In 1875, the Allingford and Winterbury Junction Railway had opened a branch line to Allingford amid strong opposition from the locals. Now, however, the line was thriving and many people who had been opposed to it had in fact come round and realised what a fantastic revolution it was. Since then, the company had been campaigning hard for an extension to the seaside town of Dillingpool-on-Sea, but in the village of Greeswell, local farmer Thomas Harwood was still sceptical and had initially flatly refused to sell a part of his land to the company. This had caused some delay. At this moment though, the Managing Director of the railway company, Charles Kettingby, was sitting with him in a horse-drawn carriage taking them from the farm to Allingford Station.

"Here we are, then. The next train to London is due in fifteen minutes."

"I'm telling you, Kettingby, I will not allow a railway to be built across my land!"

Kettingby ignored him. They dismounted from the carriage and entered the station. Kettingby purchased two return tickets to London and they walked over the footbridge and onto the opposite platform.

Fifteen minutes later, the train to London steamed into the station and the two men climbed aboard. They sat down in a First Class compartment and the train chuffed out of the station. Harwood sat in a corner, still sulking about the railway being a nuisance, while Kettingby sat looking out of the window at the countryside rushing past. These men could hardly be more different in appearance: Kettingby was a slightly rotund, bearded gentleman and was smartly dressed in a waistcoat and top hat, whereas Harwood was much thinner and clean-shaven.

As the journey progressed, Harwood seemed to ease up. In less than two hours the train had arrived in Bristol and the farmer appeared to be taken aback. Kettingby noticed this and hoped that by the time they reached London, Harwood would finally be sufficiently convinced to allow the new line to be built.

By the time they pulled into Paddington Station, Harwood seemed very excited. A journey which would previously have taken them several days by stagecoach had been completed in just six hours. As they stepped onto the platform, Kettingby turned to the farmer and said, "Well, what do you think now?"

"Well, Kettingby, I have to admit, I was wrong. It certainly is impressive being able to travel to London so quickly. I will agree to the sale of my land."

"Excellent! Now we need to get to our meeting."

They walked out of the station and climbed into a carriage which took them to the Houses of Parliament for the meeting. There had been many previous meetings with Parliament, but this one was necessary to obtain authorisation for the route. Harwood's presence was also crucial; without his permission for the company to purchase his land, the line could not be built.

"...and we feel that this line will bring excellent benefits to the town of Dillingpool-on-Sea and the surrounding area, creating many jobs for local people and providing a substantial boost to the local economy through transport of tourists and of goods."

"Thank you, Mr Kettingby," said the Transport Secretary. "But the construction of this line cannot proceed unless an agreement is reached over the purchase of the land, and you have already informed us that Mr Harwood has been very reluctant to sell, is that right?"

Harwood cleared his throat.

"Sir, I did indeed initially refuse. However, having seen the benefits of rapid transit on the journey into London today, I have come to realise that the line will indeed bring tangible benefits to the local area. As such, I will agree to the purchase of my land."

"Well, that is settled. Having heard the arguments put forward, all that now remains is to agree a price for Mr Harwood's land."

After a couple of hours of negotiation, an agreement was reached over the purchase of the land and Kettingby shook hands with the Transport Secretary, who handed over the necessary documentation granting the Act of Parliament for the line. Kettingby and Harwood left the Houses of Parliament and climbed into the waiting carriage, which took them to a hotel near Paddington Station to stay that night before catching the first train the following morning back to Allingford.

CHAPTER 2

ANNOUNCEMENT

Two days later, a meeting was held in Allingford Village Hall to announce the news that the company had finally been given the all-clear to proceed with the construction of the new line. Kettingby stood on a box to address the crowd.

"Ladies and Gentlemen, as Managing Director of the Allingford and Winterbury Junction Railway, it gives me great pleasure to announce that we have at last been granted permission to build our new line."

Cheers issued from the crowd. Kettingby then unrolled a large scroll and read aloud from it:

"By Order of Her Majesty Queen Victoria, Parliament hereby grant permission to the Allingford & Winterbury Junction Railway for an extension of seventeen miles and forty-three chains from Allingford to Dillingpool-on-Sea as of the date of the Fourth of September 1883."

At the reading of the Act of Parliament, the crowd cheered and applauded.

That evening, the conversation in The Blacksmith's Arms pub in Greeswell was animated. A group of men sat in a corner talking about the day's events.

"It seems they're going to have a recruitment event in Allingford Village Hall tomorrow to get people to build the line."

"Really, Andrew?"

"Yes, George. So anyone looking for a job can go along and apply."

"Well, I'm up for that," said another man. "I've been looking for work ever since my business closed down."

"You were running it very well, Robert. What went wrong?" asked George.

"I'd rather not talk about it," Robert said flatly.

"Fair enough," said Andrew. "What about you, Henry?"

"I'll go along too," said another man. "I could do with some extra money." He turned to the bar. "Hey, Arthur, bring us another pint!" he yelled.

Arthur Robinson, the landlord, tutted and started to fill a pewter tankard with light brown ale. He carried it over to the table and set it down in front of Henry.

"I do wish you'd order at the bar like everyone else! It's extremely rude to shout across the room."

"Oh, lighten up!" Henry shouted airily. He turned back to the others. "So, that's settled – we're all going to go to Allingford tomorrow to sign up."

"That sounds good to me," replied George.

The four men sat round the table for the rest of the evening, discussing what jobs they would be best suited to in the construction of the line. Robert had run his own business for a while, so he knew how to be organised. On the other hand, the other three were not particularly intellectual, yet they were very strong and stoutly built. Eventually they agreed which jobs they would apply for the following day. After closing time, they wished each other goodnight and went their separate ways back to their homes.

CHAPTER 3

RECRUITMENT AND CONSTRUCTION

The following morning, outside Allingford Village Hall there was an almighty queue of people looking for work. Anticipating this, Robert, Henry, George and Andrew had all arrived early and were standing at the front of the queue. After some minutes, the doors opened and the people filed into the main hall, where there was an ornate desk. Charles Kettingby sat behind it, waiting to interview people. First up was Robert.

"Please sit down. Your name, please?"

"Robert Ingleway, Sir."

"OK, Mr Ingleway. What experience do you have?"

"Well, I used to run my own coal merchants."

"Right. Sounds good – go on."

"Well, I have plenty of experience in organising people and keeping records. I can motivate people and communicate instructions to them. I think I'd be suited to be a foreman."

Robert then went on to give a lengthy account of his administrative experiences in his coal business and how this would suit him to the job of foreman. He also explained that, due to an accident which had once occurred with a cart full of coal, he would not be able to undertake any kind of physical work, but he nevertheless felt he could make a vital contribution to the company in many other ways. After this, Kettingby replied, "Sounds good to me. Welcome aboard, Mr Ingleway."

The two men stood up and shook hands.

"Next, please."

Henry ambled up and sat down in the chair opposite Kettingby.

"OK. You are…?"

"Adwick, Sir. Henry Adwick. I'm a blacksmith at the moment, but I'm looking for some extra work to try and bring in a bit more money."

After several questions, Henry was given a job as a navvy. George and Andrew soon followed him into the same role, along with many others. Some people were very confident and were offered jobs straight away, while others gave poor accounts of themselves and were refused. Eventually, after a long hard day, Kettingby was satisfied that he had recruited all the people he needed and took them into another room to address them.

"OK, everyone. As of today, you are all employees of the Allingford and Winterbury Junction Railway. I hope that you will all work together as an excellent team, as we have worked hard to acquire permission to build this line and the future of the company could depend on its success. Any questions?"

George raised his hand.

"Yes, Mr Randall?"

"When do we start?"

"The morning shift starts tomorrow morning at 6:30 at Allingford Station. I trust we'll see you all then. Any more questions?"

Andrew raised his hand.

"Yes, Mr Hackworth?"

"What will be happening tomorrow?"

"We'll give you a briefing of what you'll be doing each day. We've set out a schedule for the construction of the line to ensure that it gets built as soon as possible. Like I said, the future success of the company could depend on this line."

Kettingby then proceeded to give a broad outline of the schedule for the line's construction, before finally saying, "…and if there are no more questions, I'd like to bid you all goodnight, and I look forward to working with you all. See you at the station tomorrow!"

"Goodnight!" chorused the crowd.

The following morning, the new employees made their way to Allingford Station at the arranged time. Kettingby showed them into the waiting room, closed the door and turned to address them.

"OK, everyone. Good to see you made it here all right. As you know, today we actually start construction on the extension of the line. First, we'll show you the equipment you'll be using and instruct you how to use it, then preparatory work can get underway. If we all pull together as a team, by the end of the week we should be able to lay our first new stretches of track! Right, let's get to work!"

Kettingby crossed the room to talk to Robert, while the others filed out of the waiting room onto the platform. He explained which jobs each of the workers would do and the best way to oversee them to ensure that the work was completed to a high standard. After this, Robert left the room and joined the others on the platform, where he briefed them on their jobs for the day according to Kettingby's instructions.

"Right, is everything clear?" They all nodded. "OK – let's get to work!"

The workers collected their picks and shovels and proceeded to the current end of the line. One group began to mark out the edges of the trackbed with wires attached to small wooden pegs, while the group behind them started to dig the foundations for the line. All day long they worked hard, until they had created the first two or three miles of trackbed. Kettingby was impressed at the progress of the first day of construction and the fact that it had passed without incident.

"Good work, everyone! For a first day's work, this is excellent. See you all tomorrow, and let's hope we've started the way we mean to go on!"

The workers all bade farewell to each other and departed their separate ways, satisfied with the work they had completed in the first day.

The next day passed similarly smoothly, and the day after that likewise. Over the next few weeks and months, the workforce toiled relentlessly, first marking out the trackbed, then excavating it and laying the foundations, before laying the track and finally spreading the ballast onto it. The construction of new stations and bridges along the route was a much more intensive job and took somewhat longer to complete. Nevertheless, the work passed largely without any problems.

Eventually, the construction was completed and Kettingby assembled the workforce at Allingford one day.

"Gentlemen, I am extremely pleased with the effort and commitment you have put into building this line. Now it is finished, I must thank you sincerely, as without you this would not have been possible. There will now need to be thorough test runs of the line before it is opened for business, so another recruitment event will be held in the Village Hall tomorrow morning for anyone wishing to take up jobs running the line."

With that, he bade farewell to them all and left the station.

Chapter 4

THE GRAND OPENING

After many staff appointments, training and test runs, the line was finally ready to open for business. A crowd of people, together with a brass band, had gathered at Allingford Station to witness the event, and the platforms were almost completely full, with many more people standing on the footbridge. A red ribbon was tied between two wooden posts on either side of the track at the end of the station furthest from the new section of line, a train waiting on the opposite side.

Kettingby was standing on a podium in front of the train, addressing the crowd with a long speech giving praise to all the people who had built the line and to those who had made it possible. After many superlatives, he finally said, "And now, as Managing Director of the Allingford and Winterbury Junction Railway, it gives me great pleasure to declare this extension of line to Dillingpool-on-Sea officially open."

He took out a pair of scissors and cut the ribbon, at which point the crowd applauded and whistled. The band struck up with a fanfare as the train blew its whistle and puffed slowly into the station.

Meanwhile, at the new station in Greeswell, Thomas Harwood was talking to the new Station Master, Bernard Weighton. Both men had brought their wives and children with them, and they were getting on extremely well. After a few minutes, the very first public train to Dillingpool steamed into the station and the Harwoods climbed into it. Mr Harwood sat by the window next to his wife, while the two children sat opposite. Mr Weighton blew his whistle and the train began to move out of the station.

The Harwood children became very excited as the train drew closer to Dillingpool. Seeing how much they were enjoying themselves, Mr Harwood turned to his wife and said, "I tell you what, Emily, I didn't approve of these trains at first, but the more I see of them the more convinced I am that they're the best thing that ever happened for this area."

"Yes, Thomas. I knew you'd see sense eventually!" replied Emily. "I kept telling you what a ridiculous fuss you were making!"

"Yes, dear."

Some time later, the train pulled into Dillingpool amid much cheering from the assembled crowd on the platform. The seafront was visible from the station and offered a magnificent view across the bay. The Harwood family disembarked from the train and began to make their way along the platform towards the exit. On the way, the son stopped to talk to the engine driver.

"Hello, little boy. What's your name?"

"I'm Jack, sir. Jack Harwood. I've come here with my mother and father and my sister, Victoria."

"Oh, so this is a family day out, is it?"

"Yeah. I really enjoyed travelling on your train!"

"Did you now? Well, maybe you'll be doing so more often! You'd better run along now – your folks will be wondering where you've got to!"

"Bye!"

Jack ran off to rejoin his family, while the engine driver turned to the fireman.

"Aye, that's a charming young kid if ever there was one, eh, Zeke?"

"Certainly, Jim."

Throughout the day, several trains crammed with people wanting to be among the first to travel on the new line steamed in and out of Dillingpool. The number of visitors to the town on that day alone was more than there had previously been over a couple of months.

Eventually, after an enjoyable day on the beach, the Harwoods returned to the station to catch the train back to Greeswell. Jim recognised Jack from earlier and asked him if he'd like to step onto the footplate for a few minutes to see how the locomotive worked.

"Yes, please!" he said eagerly. He promptly climbed up into the cab where the driver and fireman showed him all the controls and the fire, which created a significant impression on his young mind. All too soon it was time for him to climb down and rejoin his family in their compartment, telling them all he had learned from Jim and Zeke.

"Father, I'd like to be an engine driver one day!"

"Would you, son? Well, we'll have to see!"

"It sounds really dirty," said his younger sister.

"I don't care – it sounds really exciting!"

Chapter 5

THE FIRST PROBLEM

The opening of the line, like its construction, may have passed by without a hitch, but it wasn't long before it was to encounter its first difficulty. Barely a week after opening, a local train from Bristol pulled into Winterbury Junction, stopping to change its crew. Jim and Zeke were waiting to take over while the locomotive took on water.

"I tell you what, Mr Douglas," said Zeke to the Station Master, "that climb out of Allingford isn't half hard work!"

"I'll tell you what's hard work," said the porter, pushing a trolley full of cases and trunks along the platform. "Moving these great heavy boxes about! Why some people have to carry so much luggage beats me!"

"At least you're in the open air, Percival. Mr Fireside has to work on a footplate with a very hot fire," added the Station Master.

"It's Wellside, I've already told you!" interjected Zeke.

"It should be Fireside – you're a fireman, after all!" laughed Percival.

"Oh, shut up!"

Eventually the locomotive finished taking on water, and Jim and Zeke climbed into the cab. The Station Master blew his whistle and waved his flag and the train gradually puffed out of the station and onto the Dillingpool branch.

The section of line to Allingford was fairly easily graded and had never presented any problems to train crews, but the extension consisted of a very steep uphill gradient just after Allingford. Until now, trains had managed to climb this gradient, albeit with some difficulty. On this occasion though, the previous crew had not made a very good job of firing the locomotive before the crew change, so it was steaming quite badly by the time Jim and Zeke took the regulator. Zeke did his best to raise more steam quickly in the few miles between Winterbury and Allingford, but the boiler pressure was still quite low and the train struggled on the gradient. The crew tried hard, but the climb was just too much and the locomotive stalled.

"Great!" yelled Jim. "We're stuck! What do we do now?"

"We're not far from Greeswell Signal Box. Maybe we can let them know and they can send an engine to help."

"Good idea!"

Jim jumped down from the footplate and began to walk further along the line towards Greeswell. In a few minutes, he reached the signal box, climbed up the steps at the front and knocked on the door. John Wooling, the signalman, answered the door.

"Ah, Mr Pottering. What can I do for you?"

"Our train has stalled on the gradient. We need another engine to help us."

"Right. I'll telegraph Winterbury Junction immediately."

"Thanks, John."

Jim left the signal box and walked back up the line to the train, where he climbed back into the cab. After a few minutes, a small tank engine arrived from Winterbury Junction. It slowly approached the stranded train and coupled up to the rear end. The train was pushed up to the top of the climb and eventually reached Dillingpool 20 minutes later than originally planned. When Charles Kettingby heard of the incident, he admitted that it was something of an embarrassment to the company, but accepted that it was inevitable something of this nature would happen sooner or later. Thomas Harwood, on the other hand, was starting to have second thoughts about the railway.

"Can't run to time, I don't know! I'd have expected better."

"Oh hush, Thomas!" snapped Emily. "You really enjoyed travelling on it last week!"

"Yes, and it was on time, like it should be! If this happens again, I shall be having second thoughts about sending our produce on the train."

Chapter 6

SOMETHING FISHY

The two fishermen sat in Mrs Headingley's cafe in Dillingpool at the end of a long hard day trawling the bay. They occupied a table near the door, eating their supper of fish and chips and discussing that day's catch.

"Good haul today, Joe! We'll surely get a good price for them at the market."

"Ar, that we should. It's hard work, but I tell you what – it's worth it!"

"That's right." He turned towards the counter where Mrs Headingley, who was quite a stoutly-built woman, stood drying teacups. He shouted, "Hey, Mary! How's about another cup of tea over here?"

"Oh, you fishermen are so crude! You come in here at the end of the day, stinking of fish, you have horrendous table manners and you can't even be bothered to say 'please'!"

"Alright then – please!"

"That's better!" She shuffled over to the table with two more cups of tea and cleared away the empty plates. "You'd better finish those quickly, I'll be closing soon."

She marched away towards the kitchen, while the two men carried on drinking their tea. Eventually they drained their cups and handed them to Mrs Headingley, who took them through to the kitchen to be washed. They stood up from the table and stretched themselves.

"Well, Donald," said Joe. "I suppose we'd better be making a move."

"Right you are. Let's get those fish over to the station."

The two men walked out of the cafe and over to the beach where the boats lay. The fish had been packed into wooden crates, lined with crushed ice, while they were in the cafe, and they had to carry them over to the sea wall. Donald walked across the road to the station while Joe carried on helping to unload the crates of fish.

"Good evening, Mr Waterwall," said the Station Master. "William Stonewell, Station Master. I was told you would be bringing the fish tonight."

"Good evening. Yes, the man who normally does it is on holiday in Penzance, so I'm doing it instead. Is the porter around?"

"Certainly. I'll just go and fetch him."

The Station Master disappeared into the station and returned with the porter. "This is Richard Warlingham – he's the porter. He'll load the fish onto the train."

"How do you do, Mr Warlingham?"

"Fine."

"My colleague, Joseph Leamington, is currently unloading the crates of fish from the boats at the quayside, so we need to go and collect them."

Warlingham accompanied Donald back across the road with two luggage trolleys from the station. At the sea wall, they loaded the crates of fish onto the trolleys and wheeled them over the road, where Warlingham pushed them onto the platform towards the waiting overnight fish train.

"Horrible smelly fish!" he grumbled to himself. "I hate having to heave these about. The sooner they can just put the boats straight on the train, the better!"

Overhearing this, the Station Master shouted, "Just get on with it! The train's due at 11:27!"

Still grumbling and muttering, the porter carried on with the job. For the next couple of hours, he collected the crates of fish from the quayside, wheeled them across the road onto the station platform and loaded them into the wooden vans on the train. Finally, after what felt like ages, he roughly slammed the door shut on the last wagon, relieved to finally be able to get away from all those smelly fish! Zeke and Jim were in the cab, waiting for the all clear to be given.

"OK, it's time," said the Station Master to himself, looking at his watch. "Right away!" he called, blowing his whistle and waving his flag.

The train whistled and gradually began to steam out of the station.

"What time are we due into Swindon?" asked Zeke.

"5:13. We need to get the fish there in time for the early morning markets."

The train travelled at a moderate speed, as the fish needed to be in tip-top condition to ensure they fetched a good price at the markets; they could not be jostled around too much in the vans. Jim blew the whistle on the approach to Greeswell Signal Box and John Wooling saw the train pass through. Wooling was just about to return to his newspaper when he noticed a shiny glint across the track. He climbed down from his box and walked over to the line, where he saw several burst-open crates of fish littering the tracks. Apparently, in his haste to be rid of the smell of the fish, Warlingham had not secured the door on the last fish wagon properly when he had slammed it shut, and it had shed its load on this stretch of track as it travelled over the points.

Meanwhile, on the footplate, the concern was more about time-keeping.

"What was that crash?" asked Zeke.

"No idea," replied Jim. "Never mind, leave it. If we don't get these fish to Swindon by tomorrow morning, they won't be able to sell them at the markets first thing, and they need to be fresh!"

"Alright then – fair enough."

The following morning, Charles Kettingby was having stern words with Mr Stonewell.

"We've received a telegram from Swindon saying that some of

PHILIP ION

the fish were missing. The signalman at Greeswell also said he saw crates of fish littering the tracks. What happened last night?"

"I don't know, Sir. Mr Warlingham was grumbling about the smell of the fish and I told him to just get on with loading them."

"Did he secure all the wagons properly?"

"Now you mention it, he did seem a bit nonchalant when he closed the last one."

"Well, I shall be having words with him – and there will be a full inquiry. Trains arriving late is one thing, but losing freight is quite another. This could damage our reputation!"

After the inquiry, it was discovered that Warlingham had indeed not secured the last wagon, and he was suspended from duty. When Mr Harwood came to hear of the incident at his farm, he was furious.

"I tell you, Emily, I am not sending our produce by that confounded line again!"

"But, Thomas…"

"No buts! If they can lose a van full of fish, they could just as easily lose some of our goods!"

"But it'll take so much longer to send it by road."

"I don't care! It's better that it arrives late than not at all!"

"But…"

"That's enough!"

Jack sat in the corner, very close to tears because of his father's shouting. He felt certain that the problem with the fish would just be a one-off incident, and that his father was making a mountain out of a molehill. Despite his father's increasing scepticism over the railway, Jack still remained determined to become an engine driver. He turned to his sister.

"Come on, Victoria. Let's go out and play."

The two children left the farmhouse and walked down the hill to the village. Eventually they reached the station, where the porter greeted them enthusiastically.

"Hello, you two! Great to see you here again!"

"How do you do, Mr Hangleton?" asked Jack.

97

"Please, call me Edward. The Station Master's in Plymouth today, so I'm in charge at the moment. You can look around, but keep out of mischief!"

"Don't worry – we will!"

Jack and Victoria spent the rest of the day at the station, watching the trains go by. Jack was in his element, while Victoria was pleased to see her brother so happy. They also looked at the plaque that had been erected the day the station opened, which read: 'This plaque commemorates the opening of the Dillingpool-on-Sea extension of the Allingford & Winterbury Junction Railway on the date of the Fourth of June 1885.' Eventually it was time for them to go home, so they said goodbye to the porter and set off up the lane.

"That was great!" exclaimed Jack, as they clambered up the hill towards the farmhouse.

"Yeah, it was really exciting!" replied Victoria, her long blonde hair shining in the setting sun.

CHAPTER 7

TWO MORE MISHAPS

After that, the children visited the station almost every day, much to their father's annoyance. Emily, however, was much more sympathetic and often asked the Station Master how they were doing. Although some of the locals were beginning to lose faith in the line after the mishap with the fish train, those three members of the Harwood family still retained great confidence in it.

One day, the children were sitting on a bench at Greeswell Station when a local train steamed in from Winterbury Junction. Jim noticed them and leaned out of the cab as the train drew to a halt.

"Hello again, you two! You certainly come here a lot!"

"Yes, we love it!" replied Jack. "My father thinks the line is a waste of time, but I think it's great! I want to be an engine driver someday!"

"Do you now? Well, it can be quite hard work at times, but it's certainly very rewarding!"

Bernard Weighton blew his whistle and waved his flag to give the all clear for the train to depart and it started to move.

"Bye! See you again soon!" called Jim.

As the train gathered speed, Jim turned to Zeke and said, "They're great kids, those Harwoods. That Jack will make a fine engine driver one day!"

"Yeah. He seems to love watching the trains at the station."

The train carried on down the line, stopping at all the stations to pick up and set down passengers. Eventually it reached the approach to Dillingpool, where it started to slow down before the station. However, as it travelled over the points just before the platform, it shuddered violently and the locomotive derailed. The slow speed meant that it stayed upright and so no-one was hurt, but it still took a long time to escort all the passengers off the train safely and to tow it away.

The following day, the faulty set of points which had caused the derailment was repaired, but many more people were becoming increasingly sceptical about the line's safety. Thomas Harwood, in particular, became ever more critical and grumbled about it for the rest of the day at the farmhouse.

"I should never have sold the land. I should have absolutely refused to allow this blasted railway to come anywhere near here!"

"At least no-one was hurt," said Jack in a small voice.

"Maybe not this time, but you just wait! Sooner or later, someone will get hurt – that'll be the end for the line, that's for sure! You mark my words!"

Despite their father's words, the children defiantly continued to visit the station almost every day. Although it angered him deeply, they never took any notice. Sometimes they would even sneak out of the house when he wasn't looking, often not returning until supper-time. On one occasion, the signalman actually took them up into his box as a treat. He was a tall, slim man, with close-cropped black hair and wore a beige waistcoat and trousers with a white shirt.

"What are all these levers for, Mr Wooling?" asked Jack.

"Please, call me John. They control the signals and the points. They're connected to cables, you see, and they run alongside the line to all the signals and points on this section of the railway. When a train goes past, I have to set the signals to show that this section of track is occupied."

"How do you know when to set the signals back again?" asked Victoria.

"Well, the signal boxes communicate with each other through

the telegraph. When a train goes past, they have to let the previous signal box know that it's gone past and the next one know that it's coming."

"You've certainly got a great view from up here," remarked Jack.

"It's not bad. Sometimes there's not much to do, other times it can get very busy if there are a lot of trains."

At that moment, the telegraph bell issued a soft 'ting-ting' sound.

"Ah, that'll be the coal train from Aberdare – that's in South Wales."

"I thought that was in Scotland," said Victoria.

"No – that's Aberdeen, silly!" whispered Jack.

The train rattled past the signal box and John pulled the levers to set the signals behind the train to 'danger'. He then relayed the telegraph bell message to the previous signal box to inform them that the train had passed through and they could now set their signals back to 'clear', before finally sending the message to the next one to inform them that the train was approaching.

"See, that's how it works."

"Brilliant!" exclaimed the children.

John walked over to a corner where there was a metal coal-fired range with a kettle on the stove. He started to make himself a cup of tea when Jack called out, "John, why's the end of that train going back down the line?"

"That'll be because – WHAT?"

He quickly rushed over to the window overlooking the line and saw that the last few wagons of the coal train had become detached from the rest and were rolling back down the gradient! Acting instinctively, he pulled some levers and managed to divert the runaway wagons into a siding and avert an accident. He then quickly tapped out a message on the telegraph to the next signal box, informing them that the train had lost some wagons and would have to be stopped at that point. After that, he collapsed into a wicker chair and wiped his forehead with the back of his hand.

"Blimey, that was close!" the signalman sighed with relief. "See, that's another reason why the train has a red lamp on the guard's van."

"What is?"

"It's to show that the train is complete. They put a lamp on the last wagon of the train to show that it is in fact the last one – just in case anything like that happens. That way, if we see a train go past without a lamp on the end, we know it's lost something."

"That's clever," remarked Jack.

"Father won't be pleased when he hears about this," said Victoria.

"Why?" asked John.

"He's been complaining about the railway ever since that train broke down on the slope. He says it's nothing but trouble, and he's been even worse since that accident at Dillingpool."

"Oh, don't you worry about that. I'm sure your father is just unhappy about the fact that he had to sell his land for it. Anyway, it's getting late, he'll be wondering where you've got to!"

He showed them out of the door.

"Bye! Come again sometime, won't you?"

"Thank you!" said the children, and they left the signal box to go home.

Chapter 8

ROCK BOTTOM

As Victoria expected, their father was livid when he heard about the runaway coal wagons. Despite Jack once again pointing out that no-one had been hurt, Thomas grew more and more critical by the day. Emily had long since given up trying to calm him down and now left him to his grumbling. Even the family Christmas dinner did little to lighten his mood and he continued to sulk throughout the day.

"Oh, cheer up, Thomas. It's Christmas, for goodness' sake!" said Emily exasperatedly.

"The best Christmas present I could ever have would be for that line to be closed down and to have my land back," he replied flatly.

"You're not still going on about that, are you? Look, none of the problems on that line have affected us, so I really don't see what you've got against it!"

"We had to give up good quality land to allow that monstrosity to be built. Waste of bloody time, if you ask me."

Deciding it was pointless to argue any further, Emily left him sulking in his armchair and turned towards the Christmas tree, then proceeded to give the children their presents.

Some days after Christmas, Jack walked down the now familiar path from the farm to the village, heading for the station. It took him longer than usual because of the snow, but he was greeted warmly by Mr Weighton.

"Hello, young man. Good to see you again! Did you have a great Christmas?"

"Yes, I did. Father's still sulking about the line, but none of us pay much attention now!"

"I see. And where's that charming, pretty sister of yours?"

"She's got a head cold at the moment, so I've come down here by myself."

"Oh, I'm sorry to hear that. Still, I hope she gets better soon. You give her our best."

"That's very kind of you. I will."

"You know, if you want to see more trains, you could go to Winterbury Junction – the next train's due in about five minutes – you can see all the big expresses go through there."

"Thanks, I'll do that."

Jack took a sixpence that he had been given for Christmas out of his pocket and purchased a return ticket to Winterbury Junction. When the train arrived, he climbed into it and sat down in a Third Class compartment, looking out of the window at the snow-covered scenery. When the train pulled into Winterbury Junction, he stepped out onto the platform and began to look around. It wasn't long before he met the Station Master.

"Hello, young man. What's your name?"

"Jack, sir. Jack Harwood. I live on a farm near Greeswell. The Station Master there suggested I might like to come here to see the trains."

"Did he really? Well, there's certainly plenty coming through here! I'm Walter, by the way – Walter Douglas. I'm the Station Master here. I can show you around, if you like."

"Thank you, that'd be great!"

Mr Douglas showed Jack round the busy station, which was much larger than Greeswell, and the young boy was in his element. Many trains passed though the station – some local services and some fast expresses. Some sped through without stopping, which Jack found a spectacular sight.

"The trains have to be very careful with it being so snowy today, otherwise they can slip and be very difficult to stop," explained the

Station Master. "Oh, here's the sleeper," he added, as a train drew up at the platform. "This is the overnight train to Plymouth. It's come all the way from Inverness. People have to sleep on it, so it's very comfortable."

Jack was intrigued by the fact that people actually slept on trains. As he watched the train steam away from the station, he turned to Mr Douglas.

"I want to be an engine driver when I'm older."

"Do you now? Well, it can be hard work at times, but if you think you'll enjoy it, that's great!"

For the next few hours, Jack and the Station Master walked around the station together, Jack telling him all about his interest in the railway, his family and how his father was becoming increasingly opposed to the line.

"Don't worry; I'm sure your father will get over it."

At that moment, the porter ambled up.

"Hello, Percival," said the Station Master. "This is Jack Harwood. He lives on a farm near Greeswell. Jack, this is Percival Burnham, he's one of the porters here."

"How do you do, Mr Burnham?"

"Fine, thanks."

"We've just been having a great chat," added the Station Master.

Between them, they recounted their conversation to Percival, who seemed very interested in Jack's desire to become an engine driver. The porter seemed to share the view that Jack's father was making a mountain out of a molehill when it came to the line. Eventually, it was time for Jack to go home. When the local train from Bristol to Dillingpool steamed into the station, he bade goodbye to the porter and Station Master, who said that he should visit them again sometime.

After leaving Allingford, the train then started up the steep gradient. However, due to the icy conditions, it started to slip then slide back down the line. Jack hoped that the signalman would notice and switch the train onto a siding, like when he saw the runaway coal wagons, but no such luck. The driver tried to apply the brakes, but it was no good. The train carried on sliding back down the bank and Jack started to become very worried.

"Uh, oh. I hope we don't crash!" he thought anxiously.

Then disaster struck. A cider train bound for Yeovil was pulling out of the Winterbury cider factory and onto the main line, just as the other train was sliding down it! There was an almighty crash and Jack's carriage was rolled onto its side. He was thrown against what had previously been the ceiling, and felt a stabbing pain in his shoulder as it struck the luggage rack. Finally, the carriages of the train came to rest in a disorderly fashion and Jack struck his head on the window frame and became unconscious.

When he finally came round, he discovered that he had been pulled out of the wreckage and was now lying on the ground with his left arm sticking out at a strange angle. A man was bending over him, anxiously looking for signs of life.

"It's alright, he's alive. I'm Dr Jeremy Banks, what's your name?"

"Jack Harwood."

"Right. Where do you live, Jack?"

"On the farm near Greeswell."

"Right, then. It's an injury to your shoulder – looks like a dislocation. We'll sort you out here and then we've got to get you back home."

Jack winced horribly as the doctor eased his dislocated arm back into its socket then helped him to his feet. He put the boy into a horse-drawn cart and started to take him back to the farm. All along the journey, Jack worried about what his father would think. He had been angry enough about all the problems with the railway that hadn't affected them – what would he be like now? He supposed he was lucky to be alive, but was sure his father wouldn't see it that way.

When they reached the farm, Emily answered the door. Dr Banks explained what had happened and she nearly fainted in shock. Once she recovered, she and the doctor helped Jack up the stairs to his bedroom and laid him out on his bed. The doctor tied Jack's arm up in a red sling and explained that he had been lucky to escape from the accident with only the injuries that he had sustained. Emily and Victoria stood in front of the bed while his father stood in the corner, his red face contorted with suppressed fury, unable to speak for his rage.

"He'll be fine in a few weeks," explained the doctor. "But he needs plenty of rest."

"Thank you, Doctor," said Emily.

"I must say, your boy's had a very lucky escape! Bye."

"Bye."

Once the doctor had left the house, Thomas at last found his voice.

"That is the last straw!" he bellowed. "I want that line closed down immediately. I don't care what you say! I want it shut!"

"But Thomas…" said Emily, in a small voice.

"No buts, woman! How can you still defend that… that… that… thing, when it has crippled our son?"

"Oh, Thomas, don't exaggerate. The doctor said he'll be as right as rain in a few weeks."

"It's not good enough. If it wasn't for that line, he wouldn't be in this mess in the first place!" He turned to Jack. "And as for you, boy, you are not to go near there again. Do you hear me?"

"But, Father…"

"Don't argue! You are not to go anywhere near that line again!"

Victoria, who understood how much Jack wanted to be an engine driver, walked across the room and put her arm round him.

"Father, please…" she sniffed, her blue eyes filling with tears.

"You stay out of this!"

"Thomas…"

Victoria, overcome by her father's shouting, put her head on her older brother's good shoulder and began to sob.

"Oh, Vicky dear, don't cry," said her mother soothingly.

She crossed the room and embraced both of her children, who were crying. She glared angrily at her husband, who walked out of the room without another word.

Chapter 9

THE AFTERMATH

If the accident had caused ructions in the Harwood household, it was nothing compared to the situation immediately facing the railway. Fearing that the company's reputation had now been damaged beyond repair, Charles Kettingby resigned as Managing Director, leaving them with the daunting task of finding someone to replace him. There were not many takers, and so many people had lost faith in the line that the company wondered if they could survive. After all, who would want to be in charge of a line that so many people now strongly felt was jinxed?

Eventually, a successor to Kettingby was found, and he was unveiled at Greeswell. A presentation was held with the station staff and a few of the staunchest locals who still believed in the line. Bernard Weighton stood on a box to make a speech.

"Ladies and Gentlemen, as Station Master, it gives me great pleasure to welcome our new Managing Director to the station today. Please put your hands together for Clement Frontman."

"Appropriate sounding name for a Director!" whispered the Station Master's wife to Emily, as everyone applauded.

"Yes, Poppy. It certainly is."

"Thank you, Mr Weighton," said Frontman, after the applause had died down. He was slightly taller and slimmer than Kettingby, and had no beard. "Good morning, Ladies and Gentlemen, I'm very pleased to see you all. Now, I'm not going to beat about the bush. The safety record of this line has been appalling. In fact, it is probably no exaggeration to say that one more serious accident could cripple it. As your new Managing Director, I am determined that will not happen. I will strive to improve the safety record of this line, starting with a thorough inspection of all the tracks and couplings." He turned to Robert Ingleway. "I trust you will see to that."

"Indeed, Sir."

The new Managing Director stepped down from his box and spent the rest of the morning talking to the people in the station.

"Emily Harwood, sir. That was an excellent speech. I couldn't agree more. My son was injured in that accident with the two trains, and my husband has been sulking about the line ever since. He wants it closed, and I've tried to defend it but if there's another accident like that one, I don't think I'll have a leg to stand on."

"Don't worry, madam," he replied. "This is my wife, Catherine."

"How do you do?" asked Catherine.

"I'm very well, thanks," replied Emily.

Catherine and Emily started chatting to each other about their experiences with the railway. Catherine revealed that her husband had always believed the line could turn itself round and become safe, which was why he had been so keen to become its Managing Director. Emily was very interested, as this was in stark contrast to her own husband's views!

Meanwhile, Frontman saw two children sitting in a corner, so he walked over and sat down beside them.

"Hello, young man. What's your name?"

"Patrick, sir, and this is my twin sister, Elizabeth. Our father is the Station Master."

"Is he now? You must be very proud of him, then."

"Yes, we are," said Elizabeth, who looked a lot like Victoria. "We often see the farmer's children here too, but one of them was injured in an accident and so he isn't here today."

"Ah yes, I heard about that. Pity. Well, I'll see you around."

Frontman stood up and walked out of the waiting room and onto the platform. He looked up and down the line, admiring the view of the station covered in snow. He was deep in thought about how to improve the safety record when the porter ambled up with his wife and teenage daughter.

"Sorry I'm late. How do you do, sir? Edward Hangleton, porter. This is my wife, Sarah, and my daughter, Julie."

"Pleased to meet you," replied Frontman cordially, shaking the porter's hand.

"Did I miss anything?"

Frontman then repeated his belief in the importance of improving the line's safety record and explained his plans for achieving this. The porter was very interested; he believed this man was the right one for the job and to get the company back on track – in both senses!

That night, Frontman visited The Blacksmith's Arms pub to get closer to some of his new staff. He was sitting at a table with some of the men who had helped build the line, and was telling them about his plans.

"...and one of my longer term aims is to extend the line to Barnstaple."

"Barnstaple?" repeated Robert Ingleway. "Isn't that a bit ambitious? I mean, that's at least another 30 miles!"

"Yes, but the current journey by train from Dillingpool is over 70 miles, on a very roundabout route through Exeter. The extension will provide a much more direct route and cut the journey down quite significantly."

"Point taken," added Henry Adwick, "but shouldn't you be concentrating on improving the safety record of the existing line before you look at building any more?"

"Yeah," piped up Andrew Hackworth. "After all, with so many people having lost confidence in the line, I doubt there will be much support for extending it further."

"Like I say, that's a long term aim," said Frontman. "The priority at the moment is very much improving the safety record, and if we can do that, it may well restore public confidence in the line to an extent that people might be supportive of the new route."

"Well, let's hope you're right," replied George Randall.

Whether it was Frontman's pledge to improve the line's safety record, or merely the fact that the change of Managing Director had breathed new hope into the locals, the line suddenly began to attract more passengers. In fact, it was soon running more successfully than at any time during Kettingby's time in office. Nevertheless, Frontman still felt that one fatal accident could be catastrophic for the company.

CHAPTER 10

DISASTER AVERTED

Jack sat in an armchair, feeling bored. Several times he had tried to sneak out of the house to go to the station, but his father had stopped him. The snow had all melted now, so there was none for him to play in – not that he could have done anyway, with his arm in the state it was. Just as he started to wonder if he would ever see the station again, the doorbell rang. After a couple of minutes, his mother called, "Jack, you've got visitors!"

Jack felt very excited; company was just what he needed. With some difficulty, he stood up from his chair and Patrick and Elizabeth Weighton rushed into the room. Elizabeth flung her arms round him and hugged him tightly.

"Careful, Lizzie! You don't want to make his arm worse!" laughed Patrick.

"I can't tell you how glad I am to have company! Father's stopped me from going down to the station, so I've been incredibly bored!"

"That's really mean!" said Elizabeth indignantly. "Where is he, anyway?"

"He's gone to market today to sell one of our cows. Victoria's gone with him to help him with it. I'd normally go, but obviously I can't with this arm."

"Could you go out at all?" asked Patrick.

"I suppose I could, but Father won't let me."

"Yeah, well, he isn't here at the moment, is he? He shouldn't be back till very late; it'll take him a while to get to the market with that cow. After all, you keep saying he doesn't trust the train. He'll be ages going by road."

"Yeah, I suppose so. I still don't want to risk it, though."

"Oh, come on, you could do with some fresh air. We can have you back here before he arrives. He'll never know!"

"All right then."

The three children left the house and started to walk down the hill. Emily, who strongly disapproved of her husband preventing Jack from going out, had consented to let Patrick and Elizabeth take him for a walk and agreed not to mention it. They soon reached the station, but after a while decided that Jack needed a complete change of scenery altogether, so they started to walk alongside the line away from the station, heading towards Dillingpool. Jack enjoyed seeing the railway from this angle, and soon forgot about his father's feelings towards it. They tramped along the route, discussing the new Managing Director and how he had vowed to make the line safer.

"…and he said one more accident could cripple the line," said Patrick.

"Did he?" asked Jack. "That's serious. Let's hope there aren't any more then!"

"Yes, let's hope so!" agreed Elizabeth.

After a couple of hours, the children reached the next station at Little Wetherington. Tired from the walk, they sat down on a platform bench to rest. Patrick had brought some sandwiches with him in a rucksack, so he opened it and handed out one each.

"You certainly came prepared!" said Jack, amused.

"Yeah. We knew you'd like to come out with us, so we packed our lunch!"

They sat there for the next half an hour, eating their sandwiches and admiring the view. Eventually, they felt ready to start walking again, so they stood up and began to trek further along the line towards the neighbouring village of Great Wetherington. Soon they reached a bridge where the line crossed a river, which was flowing very quickly due to the large amount of water generated by the melted snow. Jack sat down at the top of the steep river bank, watching the torrent of water below, while Patrick and Elizabeth started walking downstream to see if there was anywhere they could cross.

After a while, a train steamed past in the direction of Winterbury Junction. Impressed, and somewhat startled by its height, Jack listened to the sound of the train rumbling over the bridge. However, the rumble was accompanied by a horrible creaking sound, which continued even after the train had passed over the bridge. Jack didn't like the sound of it and, as he watched, he noticed the fast flowing river was pounding against the bridge pillars with tremendous force.

Then, all of a sudden, the bridge collapsed and was washed away. Jack was horrified. He looked at his watch and realised that the express train from London was due in a few minutes. Remembering what Patrick had said about the Managing Director's words, he knew he'd have to warn the train. However, he was too far from the station to get there in time. What should he do? Despairingly, he lowered his head and tried to think. In doing so, he noticed his sling was loose.

His sling! It was red! With some difficulty, he untied it from round his neck one-handed, then picked up a long stick from the ground and tied the sling to it. Quickly, he rushed round the previous curve in the line and prepared to wave his makeshift flag to stop the train. Barely had he made it round the corner than he saw a thick plume of smoke behind the trees. He immediately began to wave his flag frantically, in the hope that the driver would see it and stop the train.

Sure enough, the driver saw it and the train screeched to a halt just before where Jack stood. The driver leaned out of the cab and yelled, "Now then, just what do you think you're playing at? We've got to get to… well, look who it is!"

It was Jim. Recognising Jack, he climbed down from the cab and walked over to him.

"Hello, young man. What's this all about, then?"

"The bridge has been washed away! You'll have to turn back."

"Blimey, you certainly were brave! If it hadn't been for you, we'd have been goners!"

Zeke the fireman also climbed down from the cab and set off round the corner to see the damage for himself. As he reached the washed-out bridge, he saw Patrick and Elizabeth running down the hill. When they saw that Jack was not there, they became very anxious and feared he might have fallen into the water, but calmed down when Zeke explained about their friend's courageous action. The three of them walked to the train, where Jim and Jack were waiting.

"Oh, I see you've got your friends with you, too!" remarked Jim. "Well, how about we give you a ride back to Greeswell in the cab?"

"That would be brilliant!" said Jack excitedly, his eyes widening. Now he would get to see an engine driver in action!

"I'd love it!" added Patrick.

"My dress will get dirty!" complained Elizabeth.

"Oh, Lizzie!" laughed Patrick. "Just get on!"

With some difficulty, Jack climbed up onto the footplate after Jim, followed by Patrick and Elizabeth, then Zeke too made his way into the cab. Jim tied Jack's sling back round him before setting off. Jack sat in a corner watching him at work, while the driver explained what all the controls did. It was very crowded with the two men and three children on the footplate, but they didn't mind.

"Why is there a teapot on the train?" asked Jack, pointing to a small shelf just above the firebox doors, where there was a white ceramic teapot.

"Well, we can use hot water from the boiler to make tea! We always make sure we have the tea caddy with us before we start off each morning!" explained Jim.

The children laughed.

"Sometimes," added Zeke "we even cook eggs and bacon on the fire! Just stick 'em on the shovel, hold it over the fire and they're done pretty quickly!"

"Don't you get coal dust in them?" asked Patrick.

"No, you just stick the shovel in the fire beforehand and that burns any dust off, then it's ready for cooking! Besides, it adds to the flavour!"

Gosh, thought Jack to himself. Being an engine driver really sounds fun!

His desire to be an engine driver had now been fanned to the heat of the fire on the footplate. He was determined that, by hook or by crook, he would realise that dream – no matter what his father said.

The train steamed into Greeswell Station, where Bernard Weighton was waiting with his wife to meet the children. They climbed out of the cab and onto the platform.

"My dress is filthy!" moaned Elizabeth to Patrick.

"Lizzie!" he whispered exasperatedly.

Mr Weighton walked up to Jim to ask what had happened, at which point the driver and fireman took it in turns to tell him the thrilling tale of what Jack had done. The Station Master turned to Jack and said, "Well done! That was very brave of you. Your mother and father should be very proud!"

"Thank you! Thank you very much!"

Jack's spirits were so high that he felt nothing could shatter them, not even his father's certain disapproval that he had been near the line when he had been forbidden to do so. Mr Weighton walked with Jack back up to the farmhouse, where Emily answered the door. After she had made him a cup of tea, he proceeded to tell her all about Jack's brave action. Emily felt very proud of her son and, after the Station Master had left, said to him, "Well done! I'm so proud of you, you did a great thing! Now, don't worry about your father. I'll make him see sense about this if it's the last thing I do!"

Some minutes later, his father arrived home with Victoria. Emily proceeded to explain everything to him, while Victoria raced into the room and threw her arms around her brother's waist. Moments later, his father came into the room.

"Do you mean that you've been near that blasted railway line when I specifically told you not to? Now that's just defiance, that is!"

"Thomas, for goodness' sake!" snapped Emily. "Leave that out now! If he hadn't been there, then there would've been a fatal accident. Surely even you wouldn't have wanted the line to close at the expense of all those lives?"

"Humph! Well... alright then. Well done, son," he said stiffly.

"That's better. You really are the most aggravating man I have ever had the misfortune to meet!"

"Family hug, come on," he said, gesturing to his wife and children.

The four of them stood up and hugged each other in a ring. This was a great moment for them – even if Jack had been disobedient!

CHAPTER 11

THE REWARD

Two weeks after Jack's act of bravery, a presentation was held at Greeswell Station; his arm was now fully mended. Clement Frontman was there with his wife, along with Bernard Weighton, Jim and Zeke. Patrick and Elizabeth were also there, feeling slightly put out that they hadn't received any recognition, as it was only down to them that Jack had been there to warn the train in the first place. Nevertheless, they kept quiet while Frontman proceeded to make a speech.

"Ladies and Gentlemen, I need not remind you that at one time this line had such a poor safety record that one more accident could've spelt disaster. If an accident had occurred involving a train from London, then that would certainly have put an end to the line.

"As it is, we pay tribute to Jack Harwood for displaying an inordinate amount of bravery and courage in warning the train and thus preventing just such an accident on the date of the First of March 1886. It is perhaps no exaggeration to say – if you'll excuse the turn of phrase – that this young man single-handedly saved the railway."

The gathered crowd applauded at these final words and Frontman presented Jack with a handsome gold medal, engraved with a picture of a locomotive just before a wrecked bridge. At the top, the medal bore the letters A&WJR, while at the bottom, the date of his action appeared. Mr Weighton whispered in his ear that it was now his turn to make a speech and thank everyone.

"Ladies and Gentlemen, it's very good of you to hold this presentation for me. Stopping the train was very exciting, and the cab ride back here was great!" (Many of the crowd chuckled at this.) "However, I'd also like to thank my two good friends, Patrick and Elizabeth, because they were the ones who persuaded me to sneak out of the house and go with them on a walk in the first place!" (More chuckles were heard.) "If it hadn't been for that, I wouldn't have been there to stop the train. Anyway, thank you all very much indeed."

At the end of this speech, the crowd applauded once more. Poppy Weighton smiled and hugged her children.

"See? You did get a mention after all!" she said to them.

They cheered up a little at this point.

Jack rejoined his family and it wasn't long before Frontman and Mr Weighton came over to talk to them.

"Well, Jack. Do you still want to be an engine driver?" asked Frontman.

"Yes, sir! Very much. I want to be an engine driver more than anything else in the world!"

Frontman looked up at Mr Harwood.

"Well, perhaps we could take him on as an apprentice? He can do little jobs round the yard, get used to the railway environment, maybe eventually train him up as a driver when he's old enough?"

Jack looked at Frontman, then at his father. His eyes pleaded.

"Well..." began Mr Harwood. "Alright. You can take him on if he wants."

"Oh, thank you, Father!"

He flung his arms round his father's waist, happier than he had ever been in his life. Elizabeth came over to Jack and thanked him for mentioning her and Patrick, then gave him a hug and kissed him on the cheek. Jack touched the spot where she had kissed him and blushed.

Before long, Jack started working as an odd job boy at the engine shed a couple of days a week, performing simple tasks such as making cups of tea for the workers, sweeping up the shed floor and sorting tools. He saw Patrick and Elizabeth almost every day, and they became the best of friends. He longed for the day when he would be old enough to finally drive an engine for himself, but in the meantime he was very happy to have made a good start!

The End

THE RAILWAY ENTERPRISE

Following the demise of Wrexham & Shropshire, a businessman with a famous railway ancestor decides to try running another service. With poor patronage having proved to be the previous operator's downfall, he knows that he will be facing a monumental challenge to make it work, and hopes that the opportunity to help restore a seaside town to its former glory can provide the service with more business.

Fortunately, the commencement of the operation coincides with several important events, which result in many people using the service. Word starts to spread about its high quality and more people are gradually attracted to it. However, when a future development project requires the company to temporarily change their route, the staff worry about the effect this might have. Will they continue to succeed where their predecessors failed?

Chapter 1

ALTERNATIVE POSSIBILITIES

Wrexham, Shropshire and Marylebone Railway, often simply called Wrexham & Shropshire, was an open access train operator that commenced running direct rail services between Wrexham General and London Marylebone in 2008. These services had intermediate stops at Ruabon, Chirk, Gobowen, Shrewsbury, Wellington, Telford Central, Cosford, Wolverhampton, Tame Bridge Parkway and Banbury. However, to prevent competition with Virgin Trains, Wolverhampton was only permitted to be used as a set-down point in the London direction and pick-up in the other. For the same reason, the trains were also not allowed to stop at Birmingham International or Coventry, which was why Tame Bridge Parkway was used instead.

As the places that the trains did serve were generally not as well populated as those served by many long distance services, they struggled to attract custom. This was not helped by the fact that, shortly after Wrexham & Shropshire started operation, Virgin extended one of their hourly London Euston to Chester trains to serve Wrexham on each weekday. Many people had found it preferable to travel from Wrexham to Chester on local services to catch trains from there to London anyway, since the journey time was much quicker – Wrexham & Shropshire initially took four hours, later reduced to three-and-a-half, whereas Virgin completed the journey in just over two-and-a-half hours. Euston being more convenient for Central London than Marylebone was also a major factor.

Wrexham & Shropshire's services were extremely popular with

the few people who did use them, with great staff friendliness and catering that consisted of properly prepared meals, rather than the pre-packaged food that many services provide. In its final year of operation, the company achieved a 99% customer satisfaction rate. However, patronage was still very low – there had originally been five return services a day (three on Sundays), but this was later reduced to four, then three, until shortly afterwards Chairman Adrian Shooter concluded that there was no prospect of ever reaching profitability and the last Wrexham & Shropshire service left Marylebone at 18:30 on 28 January 2011. The company was not insolvent and all the staff were able to receive their full redundancy entitlements, but the loss was still felt by many.

*

Not long after the cessation of the Wrexham & Shropshire services, 40-year-old businessman Alan Trevithick, great-great-great-great-grandson of the celebrated railway engineer Richard Trevithick, was pondering the demise and considering possibilities. Although he had never had any professional interest in railways, he was nevertheless a very keen enthusiast – not unexpected, having such a significant ancestor! The continuation of Virgin's once-daily service to Euston meant that Wrexham still retained a direct service to London, but the sizeable towns of Shrewsbury and Telford were left without one, so could anyone make a replacement service work?

"Well," he thought to himself, "the main problem was low patronage. How could that be improved?"

He felt sure that the best way would be to try to serve places with greater population, but how to achieve this without appearing to compete with Virgin Trains?

A few days later, he gathered some of his friends together for an informal talk about his idea. He explained the problems that Wrexham & Shropshire had experienced and how they had arisen, before revealing his idea of a replacement.

"Obviously we can't serve Birmingham or Coventry because they're already served by other operators, so we have to think of some other way. Well, I'd say there's no reason that the service has to start from Wrexham, so I was thinking if we could extend it up the Borderlands Line then that might provide more potential custom."

"That's possible," put in Derek Gravesberie. "But where would it actually start from?"

"Well, with all the work that's going into regenerating New Brighton at the moment, I was thinking we could run from there. We'd need to get the chord at Bidston reinstated, but I think it's worth a try."

Alan had thought deeply about this. Decades previously, New Brighton had very much lived up to its name, being just as popular for day trips as Brighton or Blackpool, but it was now a shadow of its former self and most visitors were locals. However, the rebuilding of the Floral Pavilion Theatre had been the first stage of a major regeneration plan for the town, and Alan thought that it would be great to take the opportunity to try and bring in visitors from further afield. Also, with so many people being unhappy about the incredibly high walk-on fares from Liverpool to London, he wondered if they might be encouraged to cross the Mersey to travel on a new service instead.

"Hmm, I don't know," said Richard Davidson doubtfully. "There's still the problem of the service taking so much longer than the one from Liverpool."

"Well, that can be solved by reducing the stops," Alan replied. "If we can't pick up passengers at Wolverhampton in the London direction, then we may as well not stop there at all, so that's one taken out. Also, I don't see there's any need to call at Wellington or Cosford – Telford should be convenient enough, I would've thought. Thinking about it, I can't see why they didn't think of that anyway!"

"True," added Luke Shackleton. "That certainly would cut some time off."

"Right," said Alan. "Now we need to think of ways to make the service itself more attractive; have some things that Wrexham & Shropshire didn't."

The men realised that this was going to be very tricky. With their predecessors having achieved 99% customer satisfaction, it was difficult to see how they could make it any better. Eventually they decided that the best approach to adopt was, rather than thinking about Wrexham & Shropshire, to think about rail travel generally. What were the main things that people often disliked about travelling by train? With this mindset, they made notes of various ideas and eventually agreed to meet up again soon to discuss them further.

CHAPTER 2

SIGNIFICANT PROGRESS

Some time later, Alan and his friends met up again to review their ideas. Last time round they had all agreed that one thing many people disliked about train travel was overcrowding. They also knew this was often not helped by the apparently ever-increasing size of luggage, which often made it difficult to negotiate the aisles in the carriages, so they began by discussing their potential solution to this problem.

"So, reintroducing a separate baggage car is a possibility," said Alan. (This had been Derek's idea.) "That would certainly free up some space in the carriages."

"Yeah, and I've got a Manual Handling Certificate, so I could manage it," replied Derek.

"Possibly, but one person might not be enough. We'd really need at least two."

"Well, a mate of mine could help. We did the course together."

"I see. Well, that's that sorted. Now the catering. Richard, I believe you had an idea for that?"

"Yeah. Apparently Virgin once had certain sandwiches that were only available to First Class passengers! They got them complimentary, whereas the Standard Class ones had different ones, which they had to pay for."

"Ah, the 'First Class Sandwich' – yes, I heard about that!" laughed Luke.

"Okay," said Alan. "So your idea was that we provide meals for all passengers, but make them complimentary for the First Class

Passengers and have the Standard Class ones pay for them, right?"

"That's right – just like what I feel they could've done with the sandwiches!" replied Richard.

"While we're on the subject of catering," Derek piped up, "my cousin used to be a waitress. Maybe she could help serve the meals?"

"We'll see."

They talked for some time more. Another idea suggested was to have space in the baggage car to carry bicycles, but possibly to charge people a supplement in order to provide a useful additional source of revenue. This might increase the possibility of being profitable and would certainly be a much more attractive option than higher normal fares!

Meanwhile, the main focus was to try and see how the journey time could be reduced – after all, there was no point in providing an excellent on-train experience if they still couldn't be comparable with other services for journey time! Eventually, they set a target of trying to see if they could provide a Wrexham to London journey time of less than three hours.

Some time later, they met again, this time joined by two others – a tall man with a pointed face and a slightly plump woman with thick red hair. Derek introduced the man as his friend from the Manual Handling course, Stuart Dallam.

"Good morning, Stuart," Alan greeted cordially. He turned to the woman. "And you are?"

"Roberta Nicholls, Derek's cousin," she replied. "Pleased to meet you, Mr Trevithick."

"It's okay – call me Alan. We all use first names."

Roberta and Stuart were introduced to the others and before long were fitting in well. The discussions so far were explained to them briefly and they seemed prepared to help make the service a success.

After this meeting, a lot of progress was made and within a couple of months they had formally established their company, branded under the name 'Mersey2Marylebone'. (The services would still have to run into Marylebone rather than Euston because of the difficulty of finding extra paths on the intensely busy West Coast Main Line between Birmingham and Euston.) Rolling stock had already been purchased and this was being rebranded at Birkenhead North Train Maintenance Depot. Alan managed to achieve permission for some of them to visit the depot to see this process. They were greeted at the entrance by two men wearing orange hi-visibility vests.

"Good morning. I'm Trevor Forrest," said the first man, who had a bushy moustache.

"And I'm Oliver Dingle," said the other. "Let's show you around."

First, the visitors were taken into a changing room to put on hi-vis vests before being led into the main workshop, where several Merseyrail Class 507 Electric Multiple Units stood on the tracks. Trevor and Oliver led the way to one lane where a line of Mark III coaches stood waiting to be rebranded.

"What's that for?" asked Alan, pointing to a small vehicle that looked almost like a fork lift truck, but without the forks.

"That's to move the trains," explained Trevor. "Obviously the conductor rails can't run into the shop itself for safety reasons, so that gets coupled to the front of the trains to drag them in or push them out."

The coaches had been painted all over in a glossy purple finish, prior to rebranding. However, the process of applying the new livery was not to be by painting, but by use of large vinyl panels. Oliver and Trevor unpacked the first one from its box and rolled it out flat on the floor next to the first coach.

"This method is much quicker and cheaper than painting, plus it allows operators to design much more intricate liveries," explained Oliver. "It also saves having to have a full repaint whenever stock is transferred from one operator to another."

"I see," said Derek. "That explains how they manage to do these complicated murals."

"Yes, that's right."

Oliver then took hold of the nearest end of the panel while Trevor grasped the other end, and the two held it up to the side of the carriage to give an idea of how it would look once it was on. The surface of the carriage had to be wiped down thoroughly to remove any dust or dirt which could make it difficult for the panels to stick.

"Right – now for the most difficult part of the job!" chuckled Trevor.

The two men slowly began to peel the heavy backing off the panel. This was indeed a highly skilled job, as they had to be extremely careful not to crumple it and to make sure the adhesive back did not pick up any dirt from the floor. Applying the panel to the side of the carriage also had to be done very precisely, because if it snagged on the wrong part it would be ruined and a new panel would have to be ordered. Fortunately, on this occasion, they had positioned it perfectly and it was then carefully smoothed out to prevent any air bubbles before they gently pulled off the protective coating on top of the panel.

"This is the most satisfying part," said Oliver. "It gives us a chance to step back and admire our handiwork for a bit!"

"I see. It's just like wallpapering really," remarked Richard.

"Well, not quite," explained Trevor. "Unlike wallpaper, these panels aren't a repeating pattern – each one is designed for a specific part of the carriage."

He then explained that even the professionals can cause tiny air bubbles to be trapped sometimes, so someone has to inspect the panel and pierce it where necessary to allow the bubbles to be rolled flat before the adhesive dries.

"Yes, that's pretty strong stuff. Once it's dry, you can only remove them with a steam stripper or a heat gun, so they're not going to wear off in bad weather or be torn off by vandals!"

"Indeed not," added Oliver. "They can never get more than a few flecks off! Sometimes these are used for buses as well. They also used the same process in Canada for changing the road signs to metric measurements – saves having to make new signs!"

After the panels had been applied, the next step was to trim them to fit around features like carriage steps and windows – another job that had to be carried out very precisely to prevent having to order another panel! They also had to take great care not to damage the rubber seals around the window frames. Raised platforms were erected to allow the men to apply the panels to the upper part of the carriage, after which the orange rail strip along the top was added – a very fiddly job which required a considerable amount of skill, as it was so long and narrow.

The final step involved vinyl being placed on top of vinyl to apply the company logo and running numbers to the carriages. Oliver marked off the measurements to ensure that these panels were positioned as precisely as possible. Peeling off the top coating after applying these was particularly satisfying, as it meant the job on the carriage was now finished!

"What's happening about the baggage cars?" asked Derek.

"Well, they need to be refitted," explained Trevor. "That's being done down at Crewe. We don't have the facilities here."

For the rest of the day, the visitors continued to watch as the vinyl panels were applied to the rest of the carriages – the shed workers made it look so easy! Eventually, it was time for the visitors to leave, so they said goodbye and thanked their hosts for the chance to see the process.

Not long after the rebranding of the stock was completed, the final task to allow the service to run needed to be carried out – the reinstatement of the chord at Bidston. The line to the east of Bidston Station used to be part of a triangle of lines connecting the routes to New Brighton, West Kirby and Liverpool, but the west chord had been removed some years earlier with only a short headshunt remaining on the Bidston side. Just north of this triangle, the New Brighton line had once had a branch running off it to Seacombe, which ran through a cutting – this now being the route of the link road between the M53 motorway and the Kingsway Mersey Tunnel. When this line had been open, the trains to Wrexham had started from Seacombe, but once it closed, the services were started from Bidston instead. As a result, the western chord of the triangle fell out of use.

The vegetation along the route of the chord had been removed, so now the process of relaying the track could begin. The team of engineers who were to carry out this task were assembled at Bidston late one night, and watched as the last train of the day to West Kirby pulled into the station. There was no time to lose – as soon as the train had departed and was out of section, the power supply to the stretch of line between Bidston and Birkenhead North was disconnected. The engineers had to wait while the current dissipated fully before it was safe for them to stand on the tracks.

Once the foreman gave the all-clear, they began to remove the necessary sections of track to allow the junction to be reinstated. They worked as quickly as possible in order to have the points and crossovers fully installed in time for the first trains the following morning. After a couple of hours, they were. At this point the team moved onto the chord itself, which allowed them to leave the line clear and work through the day.

Due to the speed of the work, the entire job was completed in a single weekend and before long it was time for Mersey2Marylebone to run their first ever service! Determined to publicise the service as much as possible and attract maximum business, they had teamed up with Merseyrail. The chord had not only been reinstated but also electrified, which allowed Merseyrail to run direct services from the West Kirby line to New Brighton. This meant that Mersey2Marylebone would not have to stop at Bidston to connect with passengers from that direction. This was important, since they wanted to provide as quick a service as possible; since Bidston was mainly used as a connection rather than a start or end point, it was generally felt that there was no other reason to stop there.

Mersey2Marylebone had placed advertising posters at all Merseyrail stations, publicising the much lower prices than the walk-on fares from Liverpool to London. However, at Liverpool

Lime Street they were only permitted to have adverts on the underground Merseyrail platform and not in the main surface station. Merseyrail had also allowed Mersey2Marylebone tickets to be purchased at any of their stations.

All the Mersey2Marylebone staff were excited at the prospect of their new service and were looking forward to their first run the following day!

CHAPTER 3

THE FIRST RUN

The first train stood at the platform at New Brighton waiting for its first passengers. Like Wrexham & Shropshire before them, Mersey2Marylebone were using Class 67 locomotives as traction for their services, and had given them names referring to the resurrection of direct trains on the Wrexham to Marylebone route.

The locomotive on this service had been named *Wrexham Revival*, and behind it were a First Class coach, the buffet car, two Standard Class coaches and the baggage car, in which Stuart and Derek were waiting. In addition to baggage handling, Derek had also been given the job of conductor, so had a ticket machine round his neck to print tickets for people boarding at unstaffed stations along the route. He also had to print labels for bicycles and luggage, so that people would be able to collect them after leaving the train. To give a more traditional feel to the journey, he had been equipped with a whistle and a green flag to give the right-away when the time came.

Luggage trolleys had been placed at the entrance to the station, with notices explaining that any items of luggage unable to fit in the top basket would have to be placed in the baggage car, and that the conductor would give them labels to place on their luggage to ensure it was unloaded at the correct station.

In order to ensure that the service was as attractive as possible, Mersey2Marylebone had left nothing out. Tina Harrison, the booking clerk at New Brighton, had even been given elocution lessons to make sure the announcements sounded better.

To avoid confusion among passengers as to the fares on the service, Mersey2Marylebone made sure that the fares and their conditions were properly publicised, with a comprehensive notice erected inside the booking hall:

MERSEY2MARYLEBONE RETURN FARES TO LONDON				
	Anytime		Advance	
	Adult	**Concession**	**Adult**	**Concession**
First Class	£90.00	£45.00	£45.00	£22.50
	(£60.00)	(£30.00)	(£30.00)	(£15.00)
Standard Class	£45.00	£22.50	£22.50	£11.25
	(£30.00)	(£15.00)	(£15.00)	(£7.50)
Bicycle	£5.00	£2.50		

Advance tickets must be purchased in advance any time up to the day before travel and are only valid on the specific train for which they are booked.

Anytime tickets may be bought in advance or on the day and are valid on any train during the period for which they are bought.

Prices in brackets refer to Railcard discounts (First Class Anytime tickets are not available with a Young Person's Railcard). Bicycle supplements are a flat rate regardless of the category of ticket purchased or any Railcards held. These supplements do not apply to folding bicycles, provided they are kept folded.

Devising a timetable had also taken some time. Originally the service was planned to be non-stop between Wrexham and Shrewsbury, but eventually they had agreed to call at Gobowen on the grounds that the locals had pressed so hard for Wrexham & Shropshire to stop there. Furthermore, although Leamington Spa had never been used as an intermediate stop by Wrexham & Shropshire, Mersey2Marylebone had decided it could be a useful alternative to Coventry. The frequency of the service had been settled on as five trains a day Monday to Saturday, and three on Sundays. This was the result:

	Monday-Saturday					
	New Brighton	05:31	09:31	13:31	17:31	21:31
px	Upton Merseyside	05:40	09:40	13:40	17:40	21:40
px	Heswall	05:49	09:49	13:49	17:49	21:49
px	Neston	05:54	09:54	13:54	17:54	21:54
	Shotton High Level	06:06	10:06	14:06	18:06	22:06
px	Hawarden	06:12	10:12	14:12	18:12	22:12
px	Buckley	06:18	10:18	14:18	18:18	22:18
	Wrexham General	06:29	10:29	14:29	18:29	22:29
x	Gobowen for Oswestry	06:41	10:41	14:41	18:41	22:41
	Shrewsbury	06:58	10:58	14:58	18:58	22:58
	Telford Central	07:12	11:12	15:12	19:12	23:12
	Tame Bridge Parkway	07:33	11:33	15:33	19:33	23:33
	Leamington Spa	08:06	12:06	16:06	20:06	00:06
	Banbury	08:23	12:23	16:23	20:23	00:23
	London Marylebone	09:21	13:21	17:21	21:21	01:21
	London Marylebone	05:46	09:46	13:46	17:46	21:46
	Banbury	06:44	10:44	14:44	18:44	22:44
	Leamington Spa	07:01	11:01	15:01	19:01	23:01
	Tame Bridge Parkway	07:34	11:34	15:34	19:34	23:34
	Telford Central	07:55	11:55	15:55	19:55	23:55
	Shrewsbury	08:09	12:09	16:09	20:09	00:09
x	Gobowen for Oswestry	08:26	12:26	16:26	20:26	00:26
	Wrexham General	08:38	12:38	16:38	20:38	00:38
sx	Buckley	08:49	12:49	16:49	20:49	00:49
sx	Hawarden	08:55	12:55	16:55	20:55	00:55
	Shotton High Level	09:01	13:01	17:01	21:01	01:01
sx	Neston	09:13	13:13	17:13	21:13	01:13
sx	Heswall	09:19	13:19	17:19	21:19	01:19
sx	Upton Merseyside	09:27	13:27	17:27	21:27	01:27
	New Brighton	09:36	13:36	17:36	21:36	01:36

p – Pick-up only

s – Set-down only

x – Stops only on request. Passengers wishing to alight must inform the conductor. Passengers wishing to board must give a clear hand signal to the driver.

	Sunday			
	New Brighton	08:31	13:31	18:31
px	Upton Merseyside	08:40	13:40	18:40
px	Heswall	08:49	13:49	18:49
px	Neston	08:54	13:54	18:54
	Shotton High Level	09:06	14:06	19:06
px	Hawarden	09:12	14:12	19:12
px	Buckley	09:18	14:18	19:18
	Wrexham General	09:29	14:29	19:29
x	Gobowen for Oswestry	09:41	14:41	19:41
	Shrewsbury	09:58	14:58	19:58
	Telford Central	10:12	15:12	20:12
	Tame Bridge Parkway	10:33	15:33	20:33
	Leamington Spa	11:06	16:06	21:06
	Banbury	11:23	16:23	21:23
	London Marylebone	12:21	17:21	22:21
	London Marylebone	08:46	13:46	18:46
	Banbury	09:44	14:44	19:44
	Leamington Spa	10:01	15:01	20:01
	Tame Bridge Parkway	10:34	15:34	20:34
	Telford Central	10:55	15:55	20:55
	Shrewsbury	11:09	16:09	20:09
x	Gobowen for Oswestry	11:26	16:26	21:26
	Wrexham General	11:38	16:38	21:38
sx	Buckley	11:49	16:49	21:49
sx	Hawarden	11:55	16:55	21:55
	Shotton High Level	12:01	17:01	22:01
sx	Neston	12:13	17:13	22:13
sx	Heswall	12:19	17:19	22:19
sx	Upton Merseyside	12:27	17:27	22:27
	New Brighton	12:36	17:36	22:36

p – Pick-up only

s – Set-down only

x – Stops only on request. Passengers wishing to alight must inform the conductor. Passengers wishing to board must give a clear hand signal to the driver.

However, on this first day the first departure was the 09:31 rather than the 05:31, as this was considered a better time to try and attract as many passengers as possible – vital for the first run. Stuart and Derek worked hard to load the passengers' baggage onto the train, while preparations were being made in the buffet car. Roberta and her dark-haired assistant, Jane Jeffries, were ready for their first day on the job. Roberta certainly looked the part dressed in a black top and skirt with a white frilly apron, with Jane being similarly attired.

"Morning, Alan," said Roberta brightly, as Alan walked up to the counter to see them.

"Morning, Roberta," he replied. "Are you sure you're going to be able to cope with this?"

"Yeah, sure."

"I mean, serving meals in a restaurant is one thing, serving them on a moving train that could be travelling at up to 100 miles an hour is quite another."

"Well, I'm sure I'll get used to it. After all, we won't be going that fast to start with, will we?"

"No, not for a bit – once we get past Birmingham maybe. By the way, your name badge is on upside-down!"

Roberta looked down at her chest and noticed that Alan was right.

"Oh, so it is!" she laughed. "Dear me, that would never do!"

She unpinned the badge from her apron and turned it the right way up before putting it back on.

"Indeed not! I was wondering why you'd changed your name to 'Atrebor'!"

At this point, Tina's voice sounded over the loudspeaker:

"The train on Platform 1 is the 09:31 Mersey2Marylebone service to London Marylebone – calling at Upton, Heswall, Neston, Shotton, Hawarden, Buckley, Wrexham General, Gobowen, Shrewsbury, Telford Central, Tame Bridge Parkway, Leamington Spa, Banbury and London Marylebone. Large luggage items must be placed in the baggage car, with labels being obtained from the conductor."

"That's us!" pronounced Alan with pride, and left Jane and Roberta to their duties while he sat down in a First Class seat.

Quite a few people had turned out to travel on the new service, and many merely to see it leave, so the train was over two-thirds full by the time the departure time arrived. Richard would have the honour of driving it for the first leg of its journey – he had been appointed as a driver due to his experience in once driving the Orient Express. Once all the doors had been closed, Derek stood on the platform just outside the door of the baggage car to give the all clear. He raised his flag, blew his whistle and called "Right away!" before climbing into the baggage car and closing the sliding doors.

Richard leaned out of the driver's side window and made a thumbs-up gesture to Derek before preparing the train for departure. First he set the reverser to its forward setting, then he released the brakes with a loud hiss of compressed air, before finally giving a short two-tone blast on the horn and opening the throttle to the first notch. At this point, a thin cloud of exhaust clag began to issue from the roof of the locomotive as the engines roared into life and the train slowly began to move. People on the platform waved and cheered.

Once the rear end of the train was in motion, Richard then moved the throttle up one more notch to pick up some speed and, after the train had moved right out of the station and onto the main line, he opened the throttle out fully to allow the train to rise to its cruising speed. The Class 67 was capable of providing almost as rapid an acceleration as the electric trains that usually used the line.

The train gracefully leaned into the camber as it traversed the curve into Wallasey Grove Road, at which point some people on the platform waved as it passed, before emerging onto the embankment approach to Wallasey Village. It crossed over the A551 on the bridge and negotiated the following S-bend before passing under the Bidston Moss motorway viaduct, which was almost completely covered in scaffolding and sheeting while strengthening work was being undertaken.

"That thing has been causing problems ever since it was built!" remarked Roberta, as the train passed under it. "I'm beginning to think it might be easier to simply knock it down and rebuild it from scratch!"

"Well, you do wonder," agreed Jane.

During these works there had to be a weight restriction on the viaduct, which meant that heavy vehicles such as buses and lorries had to leave the motorway on one side of the junction, traverse the roundabout underneath the viaduct and rejoin at the other side!

Shortly after this, the train reached the triangular junction with the West Kirby line, where it rounded the newly-reinstated chord to pass through Bidston before immediately deviating onto the Borderlands Line; houses were to the left of the direction of travel and the M53 motorway to the right. Richard slowed the train for the approach to Upton, but there were no passengers waiting on this occasion and so it sailed through without stopping. After this, it started to climb the gradual gradient up to the bridge over Woodchurch Road, before skirting round the edge of the North Cheshire Trading Estate and diving under the M53. The change in scenery from one side of the motorway bridge to the other was quite dramatic, immediately swapping the heavily-urbanised outskirts of Birkenhead for rolling green fields. However, almost as immediately, the line disappeared into a grassy cutting, emerging several minutes later on the embankment approaching Heswall.

Like at Upton, there were no passengers waiting at Heswall Station, which was some distance from the town centre. In fact, it was quite literally right on the edge of the town, with houses immediately to the right and fields immediately to the left. Neston, on the other hand, is much more central, and consequently there were several people waiting there – including two with bicycles – so the train made its first intermediate stop. Derek issued the two cyclists with tickets for themselves and labels for their bicycles, which he looped round the handlebars before stowing them in the special racks in the baggage car.

The baggage cars had been refitted in an excellent manner. The vestibules at either end had been removed and replaced with sliding doors in the centre of the carriage, while all the windows had been covered over. Shelves had been installed along the full length of the carriage to hold luggage, while at the bottom one side had been equipped with racks to hold bicycles. The racks in each half of the carriage were on opposite sides to each other, so that from the door area the rack facing in front was on the left, with the other side being used for baggage. They could also be retracted if necessary, so there would be more baggage space in the event of it being needed.

Because the train had not had to stop at Upton or Heswall, it was slightly early arriving at Neston. Derek had to wait a couple of minutes before giving the right away, since trains have to stick to their allotted slot in the schedule to avoid causing problems for other trains. Eventually, the train pulled out of the station and Derek set off down the carriages to issue tickets to the other passengers who had boarded at Neston. Before long, another cutting was entered – this time a deep sandstone one with near-vertical sides. Once the train emerged from the cutting, the passengers were treated to a spectacular view across the Dee Estuary, before they crossed the border into Wales.

The train slowed down on the approach to the sidings at Dee Marsh Junction and passed through the small halt at Hawarden Bridge, which trains only called at two or three times a day to serve the Deeside Industrial Park, before crossing the bowstring bridge over the River Dee and passing over the North Wales Coast Line as it entered Shotton High Level.

After the stop at Shotton, *Wrexham Revival* began to climb up into the mountains. There were no passengers waiting at Hawarden so the train passed straight through, while Buckley was also devoid of any people wishing to board. At this point, Richard opened the throttle out further, as there were no more stops before Wrexham. Jane and Roberta had already started making breakfast for the passengers as soon as the train had left New Brighton, and now they began serving. Roberta proved to be just as capable of serving meals on the move as she had been in a stationary restaurant, managing to counteract the motion of the train effectively as it travelled along and eventually pulled into Wrexham General.

"Well, now we're travelling over old territory," said Derek to Stuart, after giving the all-clear to leave Wrexham.

"Yes, indeed we are. Will we be able to do it in less than three hours from here, do you think?"

"Well, the timetable has been carefully planned to allow us to. Hopefully we'll manage it."

Only a handful of passengers boarded the train at Gobowen, but the two cyclists who had joined at Neston left the train after collecting their bicycles from the baggage car. The semaphore-signalled approach to Shrewsbury was cautious as the significant number of routes converging at the station contrived to make it the busiest station in Shropshire, and Derek and Stuart were kept busy loading baggage onto the train due to the high number of passengers boarding it at this point. Richard climbed down from the cab and was replaced by the relief driver, Hugh Harlech.

After the right-away had been given, the train started up again and rounded the curve to take the line towards Wolverhampton, passing Severn Bridge Junction Signal Box – the largest working mechanical signal box in the world, following the closure of Spencer Street No. 1 box in Melbourne earlier that year. Once clear of the station approach, Hugh accelerated the train up to the line speed and before long it was passing through Wellington without stopping. After negotiating the tunnel at Oakengates, the train began to slow down again for the approach to Telford Central.

Although Telford itself is a New Town, the general area is largely accepted as being the birthplace of the Industrial Revolution – particularly surrounding places such as Coalbrookdale and Ironbridge. (The town is named after Thomas Telford – aka 'The Colossus of Roads' – one of the Industrial Revolution's most important pioneers.) Alan Trevithick smiled as the train pulled into Telford Central, thinking of how his famous great-great-great-great-grandfather had built a steam locomotive at Coalbrookdale in 1803. Since there is no proof that this loco ever ran, the one that he built a year later at Penydarren, near Merthyr Tydfil, is generally accepted as the world's first working locomotive. There is no record of exactly what the Penydarren engine looked like, but it is usually portrayed as being the same as the Coalbrookdale one, the reasoning being that at such an early stage the design was hardly likely to have been altered significantly in the course of a year. (In 2004, the Royal Mint produced a special £2 coin embossed with an image of the locomotive to help mark the 200th anniversary of its first run – quite ironic considering that its inventor died in poverty!)

These early locos did not have flanged wheels running on raised rails like modern trains, but instead used flat-rimmed wheels which ran along an L-shaped 'plateway'. As part of the 2004 celebrations, the National Railway Museum in York built a working replica of the Penydarren locomotive, which also required laying a plateway for it to run on – almost certainly the first brand new such route since the first run!

By the time the train passed through Wolverhampton, again without stopping, most of the passengers who had been served breakfast had finished and Luke Shackleton, who had been given the job of attending the tea trolley, was making his way down the train collecting up the plates and cutlery.

"How are we doing for time, Alan?" he asked, as he collected Alan's used plate from him.

"Pretty well, actually," came the reply. "We were a bit late leaving Shrewsbury because of the extra baggage, but we managed to make it up by the time we got to Telford."

"Excellent. I tell you what, that baggage car certainly makes a difference – it's much easier to get the trolley down the aisle without having the way constricted by all those protruding bags!"

"I can imagine! That's one of the main reasons we came up with the idea."

"Well, I must say, it's been a great one."

Luke continued to collect the plates and cutlery from the passengers before taking them through to the buffet car, where Jane and Roberta began to wash up.

Tame Bridge Parkway provided a handful of passengers, while Leamington Spa had a number of people who had travelled down from Coventry. After this, the train was able to run at almost its maximum speed, only slowing for the junction at Fenny Compton. By the time the final pick-up at Banbury was made, all the staff felt very confident and extremely pleased with how well this first run had panned out.

At last, Derek's voice sounded over the public address system announcing that the train would shortly be arriving into Marylebone, reminding passengers to take all their personal belongings with them when leaving the train, including any items of luggage that had been stowed in the baggage car. Sure enough, the train gradually slowed down as it travelled through the tunnels on the approach to the former Great Central terminus, then it coasted into its allotted berth and finally came to rest just short of the buffers.

"Well, how are we for time?" asked Stuart.

"We're right on time!" exclaimed Derek, as he checked his watch.

"Brilliant. That means we *can* do Wrexham to London in less than three hours!"

"Yeah, the only question now is whether we can achieve that regularly."

Meanwhile, in the buffet car Alan was addressing the others. First came the announcement that they had arrived on time, then congratulations for the job they had done.

"Well done, ladies," he said to Jane and Roberta. "You did an excellent job – keep it up! If we carry on like this, hopefully word will get round and more people will want to travel with us!"

Overall, the staff felt that this first run had been a great success and were determined to prove to all the sceptics that Merseyside could indeed justify having two direct services to London!

CHAPTER 4

THE CHRISTMAS RUSH

During the summer, Mersey2Marylebone attracted a great deal of custom. In addition to the service being advertised at all Merseyrail stations, New Brighton was also publicised at all the stations served by it, with the result that many people along the route visited the town on day trips. Alan's suggestion that word about the service might spread and attract more people to travel with them appeared to come true, and passengers often made positive comments about the journey when they travelled. The baggage car certainly made a difference to the space and, although the idea of having to stow luggage in a separate carriage wasn't popular with everyone, most people appreciated the extra room, particularly when they considered the enormous size of some luggage items!

By the time the Christmas holiday period arrived, the baggage car really began to prove its worth, due to the large number of people travelling away for Christmas and the extra baggage this generated. Mersey2Marylebone erected notices to explain that they would not be carrying bicycles (except for folding ones) over this period, in order to have more room for baggage, with the bicycle racks being retracted. Finally, on Christmas Eve the 09:31 to Marylebone was waiting to depart from New Brighton and all the staff were starting to get in the holiday mood, with Jane and Roberta wearing sprigs of holly in their hair. Once the departure time arrived, Derek gave the right-away and the train started off.

"Morning, Alan," said Roberta brightly, as she approached his table, where he sat with his wife, Davina; their 13-year-old son,

Matthew; and 10-year-old daughter, Amelia. Like the staff, they were getting in the Christmas mood.

"Morning, Roberta," he replied, before introducing his family to her.

"Pleased to meet you, I'm sure."

Hugh Harlech was off duty today, and sat at the table opposite with his wife, Megan. Like Alan and his family, they were travelling to London for Christmas and were looking forward to it. Although it was very cold, there was hardly any snow about to start with.

"See, that's the thing with Merseyside," said Alan to Hugh. "We're very well protected with being surrounded by the Irish Sea, the Pennines and the Welsh hills. If we get any sort of snow at all, you can bet your bottom dollar that the rest of the country will be smothered in it!"

"That's true," Hugh agreed. "Let's just hope that there isn't much on the way to hold us up!"

After the stops at Upton, Heswall and Neston, the train crossed over the River Dee and into Shotton, before starting the climb up to Hawarden. At this point, snow did start to become more prominent, so Richard had to use the sanders to help the train start up from the stops at Hawarden and Buckley. The run after Wrexham was fairly cautious because of the weather, and consequently the train arrived at Shrewsbury a couple of minutes late. There were also a lot of people boarding, meaning that there was a lot of baggage for Derek and Stuart to handle, so the train set off several minutes behind.

After Leamington Spa, the weather continued to affect the train's punctuality. Earlier in the day the line had been blocked by heavy snowdrifts, and although these had now been cleared, many trains on the line ahead were still delayed as a result, and there were numerous signal checks. This caused the train to arrive at Banbury 20 minutes late. Once it departed, the line fortunately seemed much clearer and the service was able to regain seven minutes of lost time between Banbury and Marylebone.

"Well, we're a bit late, but it is winter and it's the run-up to

Christmas, so I suppose that's only to be expected," Alan observed, as the passengers prepared to leave the train.

He wished the others a Merry Christmas and led his family onto the platform, while the staff began to prepare the train for the return journey. Since it was Christmas Eve, the 21:46 would not be running, so the last train of the day would be the 17:46 – due into New Brighton at 21:36.

By the time this last train departed from Marylebone, it was nearly dark and the Christmas spirit was starting to run deep. The worst of the delays on other services had now been made up and the train had a clear run to Banbury and Leamington Spa, where only a handful of people left. As on the way down, there were many passengers on the train, but hardly any boarded at the intermediate stops – nearly all of them seemed to be setting down passengers, possibly travelling home for Christmas. Arrival at Shrewsbury was in complete darkness and there was a long wait while the baggage was unloaded. The large number of passengers who had alighted stood shivering in the cold on the platform while Derek gave the right-away and the train slowly began to pull out of the station.

There were similar scenes at Wrexham, where no passengers boarded, then the train started on its final stretch up the Borderlands Line. Buckley was passed without stopping, while only a handful of people left at the other intermediate stops. After Derek had unloaded a few items from the baggage car at Upton for the small number of passengers leaving there, he once more blew his whistle and waved his flag to start the train on the very last leg of its journey. Having given this final signal, he felt somewhat relieved and he and Stuart began to relax as the train passed through Bidston and slowly traversed the curve to the New Brighton branch. Once they reached their destination, they started preparing themselves.

"Well, Stuart," said Derek. "Home again! Just need to get this lot unloaded and then we can start enjoying Christmas!"

He gestured towards the remaining baggage items.

"Sure," replied Stuart. "Well, let's get started. The sooner we start, the sooner we can get off!"

The remaining passengers lined up outside the baggage car to retrieve their luggage from Derek and Stuart, who wished each and every one of them a Merry Christmas and hoped that they'd had a pleasant journey. Eventually, the last passengers left the station and the two men made a quick double-check to make sure no luggage items had been left behind, before they stepped out onto the platform. Jane and Roberta were already walking towards the exit.

"Merry Christmas!" they called.

"Same to you!" was the cheerful reply.

Roberta stopped to give her cousin a hug and say that she would look forward to seeing him again after Christmas. With this, the four of them left the station and went their separate ways.

CHAPTER 5

UP FOR THE CUP

Not long after Christmas, Mersey2Marylebone's first AGM revealed that they had achieved 98% punctuality in their first year of operation.

"That's amazing!" exclaimed Roberta.

"Indeed it is," agreed Alan. "Unsurprisingly, the other 2% was mainly during the run-up to Christmas."

"That's understandable," said Stuart. "The weather and large volume of passengers certainly played a part."

A couple of months into the year, Tranmere Rovers had fought their way through to the Third Round of the FA Cup and landed a glamorous tie away to Chelsea. Shortly after the Third Round draw had been made, it was announced that Mersey2Marylebone would run an additional special service to London to take fans to the game.

"Oh, no!" groaned Roberta, who had never been remotely interested in football and was dreading the prospect of serving rowdy supporters on the journey. She had already had some experience of this when some fans had used the service to travel to the First Round tie away to Telford United – Tranmere had comfortably won 6-1 – but to have a whole train full of them was not something she wanted to put up with!

The special train was to leave New Brighton at 10:00, and would only stop at Upton, Heswall and Neston. There would be no baggage car on this service, since it was figured that the supporters were unlikely to be carrying any bulky luggage items. Instead, an extra passenger carriage would be attached to maximise the number of people that could be carried. For the same reason, there were no First Class carriages either. All tickets for the service were to be given to the club to sell to people who wished to purchase them along with their match tickets, so that Stuart and Derek could check them before people boarded the train.

Eventually the day of the game arrived and, following Derek's whistle, the train departed from New Brighton. Roberta was dreading the journey, but everyone else was well prepared. The three intermediate stops were longer than usual because all the tickets had to be checked before everyone boarded, but this time was soon cancelled out by the fact that there would be no further stops. Being a special train, other services would be given priority, so plenty of slack had to be built into the timetable to allow for signal checks and pathing requirements. The train stopped at Telford to allow Richard Davidson to hand over the controls to Hugh, but this was the one station stop besides the pick-ups.

As Roberta had dreaded, the fans gradually became rowdier as the train travelled further south, and she was relieved when they finally pulled into Marylebone and they all left the train to find their way to Stamford Bridge.

"I'm worn out after all that!" she sighed to Jane, once the train was empty except for the staff. "I'm going to need a stiff brandy to recover!"

She poured herself a glass of brandy from the bar behind the counter – which had not been operational during the journey, for obvious reasons – entered it into the till and put the money in, before making her way through to the next carriage, while the rest of the staff settled round the radio to listen to the match. Roberta could hear them getting very excited as the match progressed, but continued to sit on her own at a table, sipping the brandy. Eventually, Derek arrived from the buffet car and approached her.

"Thought you looked a bit bored sitting there on your own," he said. "You all right?"

"Yeah, I'm fine, thanks. Just a bit worn out. How's it going, anyway?"

She wasn't particularly bothered about knowing the answer to this question, but thought it polite to ask anyway.

"It's half-time – Chelsea are a goal up."

"Oh."

Derek sat down next to his cousin and put an arm round her briefly. Even when the second half started, he continued to sit with her to keep her company, which she greatly appreciated. They sat together while the rest of the staff continued to listen to the match on the radio, until eventually a loud cheer issued from the buffet car.

"Oh, sounds like something's happened!" Derek said excitedly, and rejoined the others to find out.

It turned out that Tranmere had equalised with the last kick of the game to make the score 1-1, which would mean a replay. Derek quickly rejoined Roberta and relayed the news to her, which she clearly wasn't interested in knowing, before they began to prepare the train for the return journey.

Just over an hour after the final whistle, the train was heading northwards with the ecstatic Tranmere fans on board, many of them singing and cheering very loudly in celebration at the result. Roberta sat behind the counter, leaning her head on one hand.

"I really don't understand what they're making such a big fuss about," she said to Jane at one point. "They only drew – it's not as if they've won the Cup!"

"Well, for them it is a very good result," Jane replied.

"I can't see why. They didn't win."

"Roberta, you're just showing your ignorance. For a side like Tranmere, holding the likes of Chelsea to a draw away from home is quite an achievement!"

"You're sounding like my brother. Every time I ask him what all the fuss is about, he always says, 'You don't understand'."

"Probably because you don't. Take my advice – if you don't understand football, don't try to pretend you do, because sooner or later you'll just end up embarrassing yourself!"

Roberta didn't feel she had the energy to argue any further, so she kept quiet for the rest of the journey – more than could be said for the fans! They kept singing and shouting, many of them standing up and twirling their scarves around. As a result she was very relieved when, after what seemed like an eternity, the train arrived back at New Brighton. She said goodbye to the others before heading out of the station and walking the short distance to the house she shared with her younger sister.

"Hi, Roberta!" her sister said brightly, as she entered the front room. "How was it today?"

"Terrible!" came the reply. "I'm absolutely shattered! I tell you what, Maisie, spending all day with a train-load of rowdy football supporters who think they can sing is most definitely not my cup of tea!"

"Oh, right. Well, speaking of cups of tea, would you like one?"

"No, thanks. I'm just going to go straight to bed. I've got a splitting headache."

"OK, then. Well, see you in the morning."

"Goodnight."

Roberta disappeared up the stairs, while Maisie made herself a cup of tea before retiring to bed.

The following morning all the staff were assembled at New Brighton for the first train of the day, when Alan approached Jane.

"Okay, Jane. It seems that Roberta isn't feeling well this morning, so she won't be in today."

"I'm not surprised. Yesterday really was quite draining. She seemed worn out towards the end!"

"Yeah, I think we were all rushed off our feet! Anyway, are you sure you can manage the buffet car on your own?"

"Yeah, I'll be fine. It's Sunday, so it shouldn't be that busy."

A few minutes later, Derek and Stuart were loading baggage onto the train, when a man approached them.

"Hello, Derek!" he said brightly, shaking his hand.

"Hi, Clive! Great to see you, mate!"

Derek started telling Clive all about how he was really enjoying working on the service, and how it was proving to be a great success, when Alan approached them.

"Ah yes, this is Alan, our boss. Alan, this is Clive Nicholls, my cousin."

"Yeah, Roberta's my sister," Clive added.

"I see," remarked Alan. "Well, apparently she's not feeling very well, so she isn't working today."

"Oh dear, what a pity. I was hoping to see her in action! Hope she gets better soon, anyway!"

"Yeah, maybe there will be another time."

At 08:31, the train departed on its journey, Clive sitting with Alan talking about how the service began. Alan recounted how he had been very disappointed when Wrexham & Shropshire had ceased operation, how he had wanted to revive the service, how he had felt it would be an opportunity to help revitalise New Brighton, and much more. Clive was very interested in all this and frequently remarked on what an excellent service they seemed to be providing.

Further on in the journey, talk eventually switched to the previous day's events. Alan recounted to Clive how hectic the running of the train had been and how the racket the travelling fans made had been a very testing experience. Clive soon began to understand why Roberta wasn't working today! Having two older sisters, neither of whom shared his passion for football, had often made life difficult for him when they were growing up.

"She really hasn't got a clue about football," he said to Alan, after they had left Telford Central.

"You can say that again!" added Jane, as she reached their table on her way to collect up the used breakfast plates and cutlery. "She reckoned yesterday's result wasn't worth celebrating because they only drew!"

"Aye, that sounds like my sister all right! She really does need a man in her life – she's 30 now and still hasn't found anyone!"

"Well, we're going to have to do it all over again in a couple of weeks. We're running another special for the replay, bringing the Chelsea fans."

"Well, good luck. If it's anything like yesterday, you'll need it!"

Within a couple of days, Roberta was back to her usual self and once again behind the counter, even though she was dreading the prospect of the up-and-coming special for the replay. She made several comments about how she didn't see why they couldn't finish the tie off the first time round and why they should have to play again. Jane didn't even try to explain, and they continued with their usual jobs.

Eventually, the day of the cup replay arrived. The special train was to leave Marylebone at 15:00, with pick-ups between there and Banbury. It would then be non-stop to Upton, from where buses would take the supporters to the ground. As on the previous occasion, there was no baggage car on the train – its place being taken by an extra passenger carriage – and no First Class accommodation. Once Derek gave the right-away, they began to pull out of the station and within a few minutes made the first of their additional pick-ups at Wembley Stadium, where a great number of fans boarded. Fortunately for Roberta, they seemed more civilised than the Tranmere fans on the other train a couple of weeks previously, and she felt slightly more relaxed.

"Yes, the west end of London is very different to the north end of Birkenhead!" Jane chuckled at one point.

Further pick-ups were made at Denham, Gerrards Cross, High Wycombe and Princes Risborough before the final intermediate stop at Banbury. The rest of the journey was made cautiously, since scheduled trains were again given priority over the special. After changing drivers at Telford, the line seemed much clearer. Once the train reached Upton, the fans began to disembark and make their way up the pedestrian ramp to the main road. For scheduled services, Upton provided a convenient interchange point with the 437 bus, which served all the places between West Kirby and Birkenhead not covered by the railway, and now several special buses were lined up by the station to take the fans to Prenton Park for the game. The staff made a quick check of the train to make sure that no passengers were left on it before running empty to Birkenhead North, where they began the process of preparing for the return journey.

"You know, normally I wouldn't be bothered, but I hope Tranmere win tonight," said Roberta. "If Chelsea win, I just don't think I could stand the noisy celebrations all the way back to London so late at night!"

"I shouldn't think you'll have much to worry about," replied Alan. "Whatever happens, it'll be so late by the time the game finishes that they'll probably be asleep for most of the journey anyway!"

The train had been parked in the little-used platform on the northern side of Birkenhead North Station, so the staff could easily move from one end of the train to the other without having to walk through the carriages. This arrangement worked very well and allowed them to finish the job much more quickly than if it had been placed in the depot. Once they had finished, they gathered in the buffet car to listen to the match on the radio. Surprisingly, Tranmere defended extremely well throughout the first half and restricted Chelsea's scoring opportunities greatly, with the result that by half-time the game was still goalless.

In the second half, the home side became more confident and started to attack more, but still couldn't find a breakthrough. Despite their best efforts, neither side could break the other down, and consequently the second half failed to produce any goals either.

"Well, we're in for a late night tonight everyone!" pronounced Derek, as the first period of extra time began.

Extra time still wasn't enough to separate the sides, and now everyone was feeling very nervous.

"There's nothing worse than having to listen to a penalty shoot-out on the radio!" Luke Shackleton breathed, as Tranmere prepared to take the first kick.

"You can say that again!" agreed Derek.

At this point, Alan put a finger to his lips and gestured to the others to be quiet while the penalty was taken.

The staff all cheered as the penalty was converted – now it was Chelsea's turn. Again they cheered as the commentator announced that the kick had been blazed over the bar. Both sides converted each of their next two penalties, but Tranmere's fourth penalty was saved and Chelsea's was scored to put the sides level. The home side then converted their fifth penalty to bring the shoot-out to match point and leave Chelsea needing to score to stay in the game. All the staff kept quiet with their arms round each other as the taker stepped up for the crucial kick. They held their breath as he made his run-up… then jumped up in celebration as it was announced that it had been saved! Defying everyone's expectations, Tranmere had won the shoot-out 4-3 and were through to a Fourth Round tie at home to Newcastle United.

"Brilliant! What an excellent result!" exclaimed Luke.

"Yeah. I don't think anyone would've predicted that!" agreed Stuart.

"Well, that's that," sighed Roberta with relief. "Now let's get ready."

A Merseyrail service to West Kirby had just departed from Birkenhead North, so the train had to wait a few minutes until the line was clear. Once the all-clear was given, Richard started the locomotive up and began to drive the train onto the main line. They arrived at Upton to witness the platform full of clearly disappointed Chelsea fans, who climbed aboard the train without much fuss. Once the last busloads were on the train, Derek blew his whistle and waved his flag and they started off. As Roberta had hoped, the Chelsea fans were very subdued on the return journey. Also, as Alan had predicted, most of them spent much of it asleep! Consequently, the staff had an easy run, which was just as well, because it was early morning by the time they finally reached Marylebone.

Chapter 6

OLYMPIC SPECIALS

That summer provided Mersey2Marylebone with a great deal of business, because many people were travelling to London to various events celebrating the Queen's Diamond Jubilee. Before long, Alan announced to the rest of the staff that they were just about to be provided with even more patronage.

"Yeah, with the London Olympics this year, we're going to run extra trains to take people to the events!"

"That sounds exciting," said Roberta enthusiastically.

"It certainly is! Well, we can't increase the length of the trains because of the platform lengths at New Brighton, so we're going to increase the number of trains. Instead of the usual five trains a day, we'll be running one every two hours. We've got extra rolling stock on hire to allow us to provide the more frequent service."

Alan then proceeded to explain other details and alternative arrangements, and warned Stuart and Derek to be prepared to handle a lot of baggage during the Olympic period.

A few days before the start of the Games, the first of the special trains left New Brighton with an inordinate amount of passengers on board. Alan was again accompanied by his wife and children, while Megan Harlech was also on board, Hugh being ready to take over the train at Shrewsbury. Because of the anticipated extra passengers and baggage over the Olympic period, an additional 20 minutes had been built into the timetable to allow for longer stops. Alan and his family were travelling to see the opening ceremony, and were all very excited.

The train made all the usual stops up to and including Banbury, the extra time proving to be crucial, but once it reached the junction at South Ruislip the route changed. Instead of taking the left-hand curve to join the line to Marylebone, it continued straight on before deviating at Greenford onto the line towards Ealing. The train then briefly joined the Great Western Main Line out of Paddington before almost immediately diverging at Acton to join the North London Line. It stopped at Willesden Junction to set down the passengers who would otherwise have left at Marylebone, before continuing to the end of its journey at Stratford, where all the services were terminating during the Olympics as it was situated right in the middle of the venue.

"So, we're temporarily not living up to our name at the moment!" remarked Alan, as he and his family prepared to leave the train, along with the other passengers travelling to see the Olympics.

"Yeah, but I don't suppose 'Mersey2Stratford' would sound right!" chuckled Davina.

"Also, people might confuse it with Stratford-Upon-Avon," added Roberta.

"Well, that too," said Alan.

All the passengers gradually left the train and collected their baggage from Stuart and Derek. Once the train was empty, the staff rested for a short while and reflected on how well this first special had worked. Understandably, not all the passengers who would normally have used the service to travel to Marylebone were happy about having to use Willesden Junction instead – at one time, it had been nicknamed 'Bewildering Junction' due to it being difficult to negotiate – but otherwise it was felt that the staff had done a good job.

For the two weeks or so of the Olympic period, the Mersey2Marylebone staff were kept extremely busy, particularly Stuart and Derek with the amount of luggage that they had to handle. This was where the baggage car really did prove its worth, since they realised that the carriages would have been badly cluttered without it!

Some people had doubted whether the service could compete effectively with Virgin Trains for Olympic traffic, but running directly into Stratford was one selling point that the West Coast operator simply could not match. With Willesden Junction no longer having any platforms on the West Coast Main Line, Virgin did not have the option that Mersey2Marylebone did of stopping there to drop off the passengers who would normally have left at their usual terminus. As a result, many people preferred to use Mersey2Marylebone because of the greater convenience of the service for the Olympic site.

All this meant excellent business for the open access operator, and confidence of succeeding where Wrexham & Shropshire had failed. Stuart expressed this one day, after one of the special services had arrived at New Brighton following another return trip to London:

"You know, with all the people using the service at the moment, word must be getting round by now about how good we've been!"

"Possibly," said Alan slowly. "But we can't afford to be complacent. We've been very lucky with the fact that we started up at just the time several important events happened to occur. We still haven't seen what it'll be like when there are no such events to attract custom."

Chapter 7

NEW DEVELOPMENTS

A few days after the Olympics had finished, the 09:31 was leaving New Brighton for Marylebone. As it passed through Bidston Station, Alan said to the staff:

"Well, take a good look at that. It's going to be knocked down before long."

"About time, too. It really is a dump!" came Roberta's response.

This was true. After years of speculation and false dawns, it had just been announced that the on-off scheme to electrify the Borderlands Line had finally been given the go-ahead. A funding package had been agreed between Wirral Borough Council, Network Rail and the Welsh Assembly Government, which would at last bring the line into the Merseyrail network.

Instead of the basic hourly service from Bidston to Wrexham Central provided by Arriva Trains Wales, there would be four stopping trains an hour – two to Liverpool and two to New Brighton. This would mean a total of 12 Merseyrail services an hour through Bidston in each direction, in addition to Mersey2Marylebone's services, thereby requiring additional capacity on this stretch. The section of line through Bidston Station would be widened to four tracks, essentially by placing the western junction of the triangle on the other side of the station. However, in order to leave enough space for the junction to the Borderlands Line, the station would have to be moved slightly further east. It had therefore been decided to demolish the old station and build a completely new one with much better facilities.

One concern for Mersey2Marylebone was whether Merseyrail running direct services from New Brighton to Wrexham would reduce passengers on their services. Furthermore, the electrification would necessitate closure of the Borderlands Line during work, which would mean a diversion, and many wondered what effect this would have.

A few days later, several of the Mersey2Marylebone staff were standing on the platform at Bidston at the end of its final day of operation. The last train of the day to West Kirby pulled into the station, bearing a headboard with the legend 'Bidston – 1866-2012'. A number of other people had also turned out to see the station's last-ever train. It stopped at the platform, but not many people boarded since they were only there to watch it run through.

The conductor leaned out of the rear cab and looked up and down the platform. Seeing that most of them were just staying put, he retreated back inside and closed the door before pressing the bell twice to give the right-away. The driver treated the people on the platform to a short two-tone blast on his horn and a wave, before driving the train away into the night as they waved back.

"Well, that's that," said Alan to the others, and they turned to leave.

They climbed up to the footbridge, where they paused to watch the train disappear into the distance. There was a feeling of sadness among the onlookers that this was the last-ever train from the old station, but they reminded themselves they would soon have a new, modern one in its place!

The following day, the section of line between Birkenhead North and Leasowe was closed, with rail replacement bus services operating between those two stations. At the same time, the section of the Borderlands Line north of Shotton was closed to allow the first phase of electrification work to begin, but to save passengers having to change between buses at Bidston, the replacement service for Shotton was also starting from Birkenhead North.

On this day, the bulldozers also moved in on Bidston Station.

The necessary realignment of the route through Bidston meant that the entire track between the station and the eastern point of the triangle would have to be ripped up and completely repositioned, and this started at the same time as the demolition. A few people stood on the road bridge next to the station, watching this process begin.

"They certainly don't hang about, do they?" said one man. "The last train only went through last night!"

"No, they don't," agreed another. "Thankfully, closing stations is quite rare these days. In any case, at least we'll be getting a nice new one in its place!"

"Certainly."

For Mersey2Marylebone, the developments meant a change of route. The services would traverse the eastern side of the triangle towards Birkenhead North, after which the line ran through a cutting to Birkenhead Park before disappearing into the tunnel which ultimately ran under the Mersey. Eventually, it would join the Birkenhead to Chester line, and a revised timetable with alternative pick-up points had been devised:

	Monday-Saturday					
	New Brighton	05:26	09:26	13:26	17:26	21:26
p	Birkenhead Central	05:46	09:46	13:46	17:46	21:46
px	Rock Ferry	05:49	09:49	13:49	17:49	21:49
px	Bebington	05:53	09:53	13:53	17:53	21:53
px	Port Sunlight	05:55	09:55	13:55	17:55	21:55
px	Bromborough	05:59	09:59	13:59	14:59	21:59
p	Hooton	06:03	10:03	14:03	18:03	22:03
	Wrexham General	06:29	10:29	14:29	18:29	22:29
x	Gobowen for Oswestry	06:41	10:41	14:41	18:41	22:41
	Shrewsbury	06:58	10:58	14:58	18:58	22:58
	Telford Central	07:12	11:12	15:12	19:12	23:12
	Tame Bridge Parkway	07:33	11:33	15:33	19:33	23:33
	Leamington Spa	08:06	12:06	16:06	20:06	00:06
	Banbury	08:23	12:23	16:23	20:23	00:23
	London Marylebone	09:21	13:21	17:21	21:21	01:21
	London Marylebone	05:46	09:46	13:46	17:46	21:46
	Banbury	06:44	10:44	14:44	18:44	22:44
	Leamington Spa	07:01	11:01	15:01	19:01	23:01
	Tame Bridge Parkway	07:34	11:34	15:34	19:34	23:34
	Telford Central	07:55	11:55	15:55	19:55	23:55
	Shrewsbury	08:09	12:09	16:09	20:09	00:09
x	Gobowen for Oswestry	08:26	12:26	16:26	20:26	00:26
	Wrexham General	08:38	12:38	16:38	20:38	00:38
s	Hooton	09:04	13:04	17:04	21:04	01:04
sx	Bromborough	09:08	13:08	17:08	21:08	01:08
sx	Port Sunlight	09:12	13:12	17:12	21:12	01:12
sx	Bebington	09:14	13:14	17:14	21:14	01:14
sx	Rock Ferry	09:18	13:18	17:18	21:18	01:18
s	Birkenhead Central	09:21	13:21	17:21	21:21	01:21
	New Brighton	09:41	13:41	17:41	21:41	01:41

p – Pick-up only

s – Set-down only

x – Stops only on request. Passengers wishing to alight must inform the conductor. Passengers wishing to board must give a clear hand signal to the driver.

	Sunday			
	New Brighton	08:26	13:26	18:26
p	Birkenhead Central	08:46	13:46	18:46
px	Rock Ferry	08:49	13:49	18:49
px	Bebington	08:53	13:53	18:53
px	Port Sunlight	08:55	13:55	18:55
px	Bromborough	08:59	13:59	18:59
p	Hooton	09:03	14:03	19:03
	Wrexham General	09:29	14:29	19:29
x	Gobowen for Oswestry	09:41	14:41	19:41
	Shrewsbury	09:58	14:58	19:58
	Telford Central	10:12	15:12	20:12
	Tame Bridge Parkway	10:33	15:33	20:33
	Leamington Spa	11:06	16:06	21:06
	Banbury	11:23	16:23	21:23
	London Marylebone	12:21	17:21	22:21
	London Marylebone	08:46	13:46	18:46
	Banbury	09:44	14:44	19:44
	Leamington Spa	10:01	15:01	20:01
	Tame Bridge Parkway	10:34	15:34	20:34
	Telford Central	10:55	15:55	20:55
	Shrewsbury	11:09	16:09	20:09
x	Gobowen for Oswestry	11:26	16:26	21:26
	Wrexham General	11:38	16:38	21:38
s	Hooton	12:04	17:04	22:04
sx	Bromborough	12:08	17:08	22:08
sx	Port Sunlight	12:12	17:12	22:12
sx	Bebington	12:14	17:14	22:14
sx	Rock Ferry	12:18	17:18	22:18
s	Birkenhead Central	12:21	17:21	22:21
	New Brighton	12:41	17:41	22:41

p – Pick-up only

s – Set-down only

x – Stops only on request. Passengers wishing to alight must inform the conductor. Passengers wishing to board must give a clear hand signal to the driver.

A few days after the work had started, as the 09:26 (normally the 09:31) was travelling round the curve of the triangle, the staff looked out of the windows to observe the work in progress. Although it was too far away for them to see, a train of open wagons – with an American-built Class 70 locomotive at the head – was parked to the west of the demolition site on the Borderlands Line. The rubble was being loaded into the wagons before being removed by train. As the Mersey2Marylebone service passed through Birkenhead North, the people on the train saw another rake of wagons on the siding running between the depot and the station, which was also headed by a Class 70. This train had travelled down from Scunthorpe steelworks, which has a dedicated plant for manufacturing rails, and was loaded with new track.

"They're a completely new class of locomotive, those – been totally redesigned from the bogies up!" Alan said, as they passed it. "They've not long been in service. The interesting thing about them is they're so efficient that their carbon footprint is actually less than that of some electrics!"

"Blimey!" exclaimed Roberta in awe.

"Not the most attractive of things, though," remarked Jane.

"Well, that doesn't matter. At the end of the day, it's far more important that they do the job and are safe," came Alan's reply. "Good looks don't save lives!"

"No, I suppose not."

"Mind you, when one batch was being unloaded at Newport Docks, they dropped one of them. The chains from the crane snapped and it crashed down onto the deck!"

"Oh dear!"

"Yeah. The only consolation is that it was the last one to be unloaded and not the first, otherwise it would've landed on top of the others and smashed all them up as well!"

"That would never do!"

"Indeed not. Imagine filling in an insurance claim form for that!"

Before long, the train passed through Birkenhead Park and

entered the tunnel. The open section at Conway Park came and went before passing through Hamilton Square, where the line joined with the route from Chester. Because of the potential congestion it could create, and also to prevent the locomotive being at the wrong end of the train, there could not be a simple reversal here. This meant that the train had to continue straight on and travel right round the Liverpool loop to access the Chester line.

The Mersey railway tunnel between Birkenhead and Liverpool opened in 1866 and was originally worked by steam trains. These were capable of managing the steep gradients in the tunnel, but the smoke from them made standing at the underground stations a very unpleasant experience, so many people still preferred to cross the river on the ferries. The opening of the Liverpool Overhead Railway – affectionately known as the 'Ovee', or sometimes the 'Dockers' Umbrella' – in 1893 demonstrated the advantages of the then new electric traction. (Electricity, like steam, had been understood as a potential source of power many years before a practical use was found for it.) Seeing how much cleaner electric trains were, the Mersey Railway decided to adopt this form of power and the cross-river route commenced full electric working on 3 May 1903, the first-ever occurrence in the world of an existing line changing from steam to electric traction.

At one time, Liverpool had three main railway termini: Tithebarn Street (later Exchange), which served destinations such as Southport, Ormskirk, Preston and Glasgow; Lime Street, which catered for most other major destinations, including Manchester and London; and Central, which served the southern parts of the city. Central also had low level platforms, which were used by the cross-river trains. The line from Exchange to Southport was electrified in 1904, and today's Class 507 and 508 units are only the third generation of electric trains to work the line since then! During the Beeching cuts of the 1960s, this line was proposed for closure, but a strong local campaign resulted in it being saved.

However, Exchange Station was closed, with the approach

being slewed to the west to run into a new tunnel. This provided a link across the city centre to Central Low Level, with an intermediate underground station at Moorfields which effectively replaced Exchange. The Class 507 and 508 trains were introduced when it was discovered that the Class 502s, which had previously been used, often struggled to handle the gradients in the tunnel. The line out of Central High Level closed in 1972, but reopened again in 1978 as far as Garston (which was replaced by Liverpool South Parkway in 2006), and was routed into the former Low Level station to provide a through route between south Liverpool and Southport. It reopened to Hunts Cross in 1983.

The cross-river line originally used to run from the underground station at James Street straight into Central Low Level, but when the cross-link between Moorfields and Central opened, a single track loop was also built linking Moorfields, Lime Street and Central, with platforms at these stations underneath the others, thereby creating the present day Merseyrail system. This was completed in 1977.

After climbing the gradient up to James Street, the Mersey2Marylebone service began to traverse this loop, which would effectively turn the train round so that the locomotive would still be at the head by the time it emerged again. There was a feeling of 'So near yet so far' among many of the staff as the train passed through Lime Street Low Level without stopping, but they could not stop there because of the obvious competition this would create with the service from the surface station. After what seemed like a long time, they were once again passing through Hamilton Square, this time via the route towards Chester. Eventually, the train emerged into daylight and immediately entered Birkenhead Central Station, where it made the first of its alternative stops. Although spending so long in the tunnels had made the journey seem a bit gloomy, the staff nevertheless felt pleased to be providing Birkenhead – albeit temporarily – with a direct service to London for the first time since 1967.

After the stop at Birkenhead Central, the train entered another tunnel, which had an open section for Green Lane Station, before emerging onto the straight stretch towards Rock Ferry. The embankment to the left of the tunnel mouth as the train emerged had formerly been the approach to Woodside Station, from where express trains had once run to Paddington. The remains of the former fast lines out of Woodside were still in evidence as far as Rock Ferry – albeit heavily overgrown.

At one time, Rock Ferry had six operational platforms: two bay platforms on the west side of the station, where the cross-river trains terminated until electrification was extended to Hooton in 1985; two in the middle, which were used by local services between Birkenhead and Chester; and two on the east side, which were used by expresses to and from Woodside. The latter two were heavily overgrown and fenced off, but the other four were still in use and it was the middle pair which was used as the train made its next stop.

South of the station, the rusty lines formerly serving the express platforms converged with the existing ones, leaving just two tracks beyond. The train began to run through the cutting, which was still wide enough to take four tracks, before emerging onto the embankment approach to Bebington and Port Sunlight. The latter is famous as the birthplace of Sunlight Soap, who also built their own private port to bring palm oil directly to their factory, giving the village its name. Today the port is disused and the factory is owned by Unilever.

After stopping at Bromborough, the train continued south and passed under the M53 before reaching Hooton, where the line to Ellesmere Port diverged. In the aftermath of the electrification south from Rock Ferry, diesel trains had run from Warrington Bank Quay via Helsby and Ellesmere Port to Hooton, at which point they reversed and ran to Chester. However, when the third rail was extended to Chester in 1993, this service terminated at Hooton, and a year later electrification also reached Ellesmere Port. Unfortunately, Helsby missed out on the wiring and most traffic on the Ellesmere Port-Helsby line now consists of heavy coal trains travelling between Manisty Wharf and Fiddlers Ferry Power Station. There are only four passenger trains a day on this line running via Helsby to Warrington, of which one continues to Liverpool Lime Street.

There were several passengers with bicycles boarding at Hooton due to its position at the end of the Wirral Way cycle route, which follows the trackbed of the former Hooton-West Kirby line (closed in 1962). Not far from Hooton, this route runs through the village of Willaston, whose former station at Hadlow Road has been excellently restored to how it would have looked in 1952. The station was so named to avoid confusion with the Willaston near Crewe – itself not to be confused with the nearby village of Wistaston!

South of Hooton, the train quickened up and before long it passed through Bache Station, which replaced Upton-by-Chester in 1984. Again, rules on competition with Virgin prevented the service from calling at Chester, so it travelled straight round the avoiding line to join the route towards Holyhead. Eventually the train pulled into Wrexham and made its stop there, before joining its more familiar route for the rest of its journey to Marylebone.

Some weeks later, the staff had just finished inspecting the train after the 09:46 from Marylebone had completed its journey to New Brighton, and were reflecting on the latest developments.

"Is it just me, or do we seem to be carrying even more people since the service had to be diverted?" wondered Derek.

"I think I've noticed that too," said Roberta. "What do you think, Alan?"

"Now you mention it, I think you may be right."

By now, Bidston Station had been completely demolished and all the rubble cleared, while the two lines from Birkenhead North had been slewed to the south as part of the realignment. The two lines forming the chord for the New Brighton branch had also been moved slightly to the north. All that remained was for these four tracks to be joined together at what would be the west end of the station and to install the new junction for the Borderlands Line beyond this point, before construction work could start on the new station. Although the Mersey2Marylebone staff had been concerned that they would lose patronage as a result of having to leave out their usual stops, quite the reverse had happened. Running through the dense urban belt down the east side of the Wirral Peninsula meant that they passed within convenient distance of many more people, so business was better than ever. Port Sunlight in particular was benefiting enormously from the extra visitors from North Wales and Shropshire, so it was perhaps not surprising that Alan had been thinking deeply lately.

"You know, I honestly feel we could do a lot worse than have a permanent service from Birkenhead," he said presently.

"You really think so?" asked Jane.

"Yeah, why not? We could keep the existing service to New Brighton, but split the train in two at Wrexham – have one bit go to New Brighton and the other to Birkenhead."

Before long, the new track layout at Bidston had been completed and the foundations for the platforms of the new station laid. This allowed services between Birkenhead North and Leasowe to resume – albeit with a temporary speed restriction through Bidston – but the rail replacement buses were still running for the section of the Borderlands line north of Shotton. The electrification of the line had been proceeding steadily, with trains loaded with lengths of conductor rail travelling from Scunthorpe to the site.

Extracting iron involves reducing the iron ore with carbon, but this means that iron drawn straight from a blast furnace – known as 'pig' iron – has a significant amount of unburnt carbon mixed in with it, making it very soft and brittle. As a result, this iron is then processed to remove most of the carbon until the right amount is left to make steel. Instead of weakening the iron, this small amount of carbon actually makes it stronger. Different types of steel contain different amounts of carbon, and the type of steel used for making conductor rails has a higher carbon content than most; in fact, it is actually closer to pig iron in composition. This extra carbon gives it better conductive properties than normal steel, but also makes it more brittle. This is not much of an issue since, unlike running rails, they do not have to carry the weight of trains and therefore do not need to be particularly strong. They only have to withstand the pressure of spring-loaded pickup shoes.

Before long, the laying of the conductor rails was approaching Dee Marsh sidings and the team of engineers felt very excited, since they were close to the Welsh border. They took their time laying what would be the first lengths of rail to extend over the border, as this would be setting a precedent. At last they were fixed into place, meaning that Wales finally had a stretch of electrified mainline railway for the first time in history.

"Have they got electricity in Wales?" Roberta joked, when Alan told the Mersey2Marylebone staff about the event.

"Er, yes, actually!" was the defiant reply. "If anything, they're far more likely to not have gas than electricity!"

"Mind you, in a major town like Wrexham they'll almost certainly have both, I would've thought!" Jane chuckled.

"To be perfectly honest, I always find it difficult to think of Wrexham as being in Wales anyway," Roberta added. "I mean, it's only just over the border."

"Don't let Hugh hear you say that," said Alan. "He's born and bred in Wrexham – very proud of his Welsh heritage, so won't take kindly to any suggestion that he's English! That'd be like saying Chester is in Wales; it wouldn't go down too well. After all, the clock tower on Chester Town Hall only has faces on three sides. The fourth side faces Wales!"

Jane and Roberta both laughed at this.

Within a few weeks, the electrification to Shotton was completed and the conductor rails were finally energised. This section of the Borderlands Line was transferred from the Arriva Trains Wales franchise to Merseyrail, who started working the line with direct services to New Brighton and Liverpool. Hawarden Bridge still only retained its basic service of three trains a day in each direction, but the rest of the stations were now served by four trains an hour – two to and from New Brighton, and two to and from Liverpool.

At the same time, the section of the Borderlands Line south of Shotton was closed to allow the second phase of electrification work to begin, with rail replacement buses operating between the stations along this section of the route. Once this phase was completed, the Shotton to Wrexham stretch of the line would also be transferred to the Merseyrail franchise, which would bring Wrexham to within commuting time of Liverpool and help strengthen the local economy. In turn, people from Liverpool would also be able to reach North Wales more easily.

CHAPTER 8

ADDITIONAL BENEFITS

Meanwhile, significant progress was being made on the construction of the new station at Bidston. The platforms had long since been completed and the other structures were at a very advanced stage. As the station had had to be moved to allow the lines at the west end to be realigned, the end of it was now in line with the road bridge over the line. As a result, the footbridge would be connected to it in a similar manner to the stations at Moreton and Meols further down the line. The overgrown concrete area in front of the old station was being replaced with a proper car park, equipped with lighting and CCTV, while an overhead walkway extended over it from the footbridge to the bus stops on the road to Moreton, and also across the road to Bidston village itself.

This arrangement allowed the bridge to form part of the existing cycle route to New Brighton, and would also make the station more accessible from the village and provide a better interchange with buses. Eliminating the need for cyclists to cross the busy dual carriageway was another significant advantage of the walkway, along with the installation of secure cycle parking on the platforms. The provision of improved car parking facilities was crucial, since the new station was intended as a Park and Ride point. As a result, it was to be renamed Bidston Parkway, rather than simply Bidston. This would also provide a more accurate reflection of its position relative to the village.

Once construction was completed, the new station was opened to great acclaim by the Mayor of Wirral, and before long was attracting much more patronage than the old one. The improved link between the station and the village itself saw many more people using it as a starting point rather than merely an interchange, with the result that once the Borderlands electrification was completed and the line reopened – allowing the Mersey2Marylebone services to revert to their usual route – the open access operator started to consider the possibility of stopping there.

"Well, why not?" said Alan, when the other staff questioned this idea. "After all, the only reason we didn't stop at the old station was because people used it more as an interchange and they could always connect with us at New Brighton instead. Now that more people seem to be starting and ending journeys there, we might be able to justify it!"

They had already taken up their plan of continuing the direct service from Birkenhead, with the siding on the east side of Central Station being converted into a bay platform for their use. This had been an excellent move, providing a steady stream of business, and Alan was very pleased with the way things were going. Thankfully, the use of the service hardly seemed to have been affected by the developments on the Borderlands Line, so patronage was as strong as ever.

Before long, the services did start calling at Bidston Parkway, which resulted in some minor timetable changes between there and Wrexham. However, overall journey time was not affected because it had been decided to drop Buckley from the timetable; most people who had boarded the train there had not travelled beyond Wrexham, and it was now just as easy for them to use Merseyrail's services.

During the two years in which the service had been running, word had gradually spread about its high quality, which had resulted in more people sampling it. Although nowhere near as fast as the service from Liverpool, the much lower fares made it attractive to many. The fact that its commencement had coincided with several important events had helped a lot. In the company's first year of operation, the visit of the *Queen Mary 2* to Liverpool had resulted in a great deal of patronage, and on that occasion the stops that would normally have been set down only in the New Brighton direction had also been designated as pick-ups to transport locals to and from the town to see the ship. A temporary jetty had even been erected in New Brighton to allow the Mersey Ferries to take people on cruises round the river while the liner was tied up at the Pier Head landing stage.

In the time that had passed since then, the Mersey2Marylebone service had brought so many extra visitors to New Brighton that plans were now being made for a brand new permanent ferry terminal there. This would be historic, as the town had not been accessible to the ferries since the old pier was destroyed in a storm decades previously. At the time there had not been the money available to rebuild it, so it had been demolished. When Alan heard about this, he informed his staff immediately.

"That's excellent!" said Stuart happily.

"Yeah. Just think – that's all because we helped bring in more visitors!" added Derek.

"Well, it's to be hoped that we can continue to do so," said Alan. "We've been very lucky so far, with there just happening to be so many important events. First there was the *QM2* visit, then the two FA Cup ties, then the Queen's Jubilee and, after that, the Olympics. It still remains to be seen if we can keep it up when there are no such events."

"I'm sure we will. A lot of people will have heard about us by now."

Within a couple of months, the stage had been completed and the ferries started serving it. The Manchester Ship Canal cruises, one of the ferries' most popular events, also started calling at the stage and these were prominently advertised at all the stations served by Mersey2Marylebone. This resulted in even more business for the operator, despite there not being any special events, and the timings meant that one of the cruises could just about be fitted into a day trip from London for anyone using the early morning train from

Marylebone. The cruises to Salford Quays took around six hours, with the return journey being provided by coach, meaning this could be fitted in between the first Down train and last Up train of the day.

Tickets for the cruises even began to be sold at the stations, so passengers could purchase them at the same time as their train tickets! Mersey Ferries had thought of this idea from the many heritage railway lines, who allowed their tickets to be sold at National Rail stations. It proved to be a very smart move, with the cruises being more popular than ever during the following summer.

CHAPTER 9

A SIGNIFICANT LANDMARK

A year after the stage had been completed, the Mersey2Marylebone services were running as successfully as ever. The staff all felt that they had helped put some of the romance back into travelling to the seaside by train – the posters at the stations, the baggage car, the traditional method of issuing the right-away from stops, and the events in New Brighton. They all felt proud to have helped restore the town to its popularity of the 1950s and 60s, which had, in turn, helped the service to be a great success.

"Well, you know what this means, don't you?" Alan asked his staff when he announced they had reached their third anniversary.

"What?" asked Jane and Roberta together.

"We've been running longer than Wrexham and Shropshire!"

"Blimey, that's great!"

The staff all agreed that this was a mark of just how successful they had been – to have reached the same point as their predecessors had reached, and be attracting several times the custom!

If the service had one downside, it was the low frequency. However, the fact that it was now being so well used meant that many of the people concerned were wondering if they could now justify increasing it. In order to provide sufficient capacity, it was felt that an additional platform might need to be constructed at New Brighton – this being achieved by removing one of the two sidings on the north side of the station and building a platform in its place, with the other siding becoming the track serving this platform. This would leave only one siding on the south side of the station, but it was felt that this would probably be sufficient. It was suggested that perhaps two or three limited-stop services could be provided, which would only call at Wrexham, Shrewsbury and Telford. This could possibly provide a much quicker journey, with a target of Telford to London in two hours and Wrexham to London in two-and-a-half.

Overall, Mersey2Marylebone were very pleased to be able to provide Merseyside with a second direct service to London – at a fraction of the cost of some of the big companies!

CHAPTER 10

THEATRE EXCURSION

Following the June timetable change, the suggestion of additional limited-stop services was followed, with three more trains being added to the timetable on each weekday. These proved to be quite popular for people who wanted to reach London quicker, taking just over three hours from New Brighton, and made the operation more attractive to business travellers.

Not long after this, it was announced that the Port Sunlight Players would be performing *A View From the Bridge* in the West End, and Mersey2Marylebone would be running a special excursion to take the theatre company and their supporters to London. Before this production, however, they would be performing the play at the Gladstone Theatre in Port Sunlight, and Alan had managed to arrange for all the staff to see it one night.

"That's fantastic. I always love a good trip to the theatre!" Roberta had said enthusiastically, when Alan had announced this.

"Yeah, it should be a great night," he replied. "After all, we've worked hard to make this service work these past few years, so it's time we had a treat!"

On the evening of this particular showing, the Mersey2Marylebone staff met at the theatre to watch the play. Roberta had told her two younger siblings about the production, with the result that Clive was there with his wife, Anne. They all greeted each other enthusiastically before making their way through to the auditorium and taking their seats in a row near the middle. Several people were talking enthusiastically, with many who hadn't seen the play before wondering what to expect. Eventually the lights dimmed and the curtains opened, giving the cue for the performance to start.

After the first act, the Mersey2Marylebone staff began talking to each other again and discussing the play so far.

"They certainly seem to be making a very good job of it," remarked Stuart. "It'll be interesting to see if they can perform as well in the West End!"

"It certainly will," agreed Derek. "I wonder what's going to happen in the second half."

"You'll just have to wait and see!" said Alan mysteriously. He was the only one of the staff who had seen the play before, but had made a pledge to himself not to spoil the ending for the others.

Meanwhile, Clive and Anne were talking. Anne was about the same age as Roberta, but slightly taller and less broad.

"It's a very interesting play, that's for sure," said Anne, who was having difficulty getting the tune of *Paper Doll* out of her head.

"Yeah," replied Clive. "Having someone as both a narrator and a character is a bit different. It must be quite a challenge having to effectively perform two separate roles!"

At the end of the interval, the audience returned to their seats to watch the second act of the performance. Most of them found it more dramatic than the first, and several of them gasped during the stabbing in the final scene. Once the play had finished and the cast had taken their bow, the audience began to file out of the theatre and the Mersey2Marylebone staff wished each other goodnight.

A few days later, it was time for the Port Sunlight Players to travel to London. The special excursion would be leaving quite early and it would take some time for them to get sorted out. So, at five o'clock in the morning, before the sun had risen and with the early morning mist still lingering, the train was parked in Port Sunlight Station waiting for them. There were two baggage cars on this train, one at each end. The one at the rear end was being used to carry props, equipment and costumes, and the additional one just behind the locomotive was for carrying ordinary luggage. Once the train crew were all assembled – some of them bleary-eyed and still yawning widely – Alan addressed them.

"Right. I know it's an early start, but it's going to take a while to load all the props and such-like onto the train and we've agreed to lend a hand. We're due to leave at 7:30, so let's get to it!"

At these words, the staff promptly moved to their posts: Derek made for the rear baggage car to wait for the others to bring the bulky items, Jane and Roberta began to prepare the buffet car for the passengers, while Alan and Stuart proceeded down the ramp from the station platform towards the theatre. It was convenient that the theatre was right next to the station, because it meant that they wouldn't have to carry anything too far. At the stage door they were greeted by the head of the theatre troupe, Eric Prowess.

"Morning," he said wearily. "Come in, we've just about got everything ready to go."

"Excellent," replied Alan. "Well, let's get moving!"

Eric showed Alan and Stuart what needed loading onto the train, and they picked up large clear plastic boxes containing various documents, such as scripts and make-up and costume instructions, before carrying them out of the theatre and up the ramp to where the train was waiting. With help from Derek, they stowed these in the rear baggage car before making their way back to the theatre. For the next couple of hours they shuttled back and forth, along with members of the troupe, transporting containers and boxes of various sizes with costumes, make-up and props, and loading them onto the train – sometimes carrying them and sometimes using trolleys. Eventually all the items were loaded and the theatre troupe began to take their seats in the carriages. Once everyone was on board and all the doors were closed, Derek gave the right-away and the train began to depart.

"Well, here we go!" said one man excitedly.

"Yeah. I'm really looking forward to performing in the West End!" replied another.

The train stopped at Bromborough and Hooton to pick up

followers of the theatre troupe, before continuing on its journey. Since this was an excursion rather than a scheduled service, the rules against competition with Virgin Trains didn't apply, so the train would be calling at Chester. As it slowly made its way across the station approach into platform 3, the staff began feeling nervous as it was at this point they would be picking up a very special guest – none other than the Duke of Westminster! Alan had drilled them all precisely on the methods of greeting their VIP, and consequently they were anxious to make sure everything went according to plan.

The train came to a stop at the platform and the locomotive was detached to allow it to run round the train, since it would be travelling in the opposite direction from here to London. This meant that the baggage car with the props and costumes would now be behind the locomotive, while the one with the ordinary luggage would be at the rear of the formation. Consequently, Derek and Stuart had to move from one to the other, in order to still be at the end furthest from the locomotive. Alan and Roberta stepped out of the buffet car and stood either side of the door, waiting to greet the Duke.

A few moments later, the Duke arrived and Alan shook his hand as he approached, giving him a small nod.

"Good morning, Your Grace," he said politely. "I'm Alan Trevithick. I hope you have a pleasant journey with us this morning."

"Good morning, Mr Trevithick," replied the Duke.

"This is Roberta Nicholls. She'll be running the buffet car today."

"Good morning, Sir," greeted Roberta with a smile, shaking the Duke's hand and giving a small curtsey.

"Good morning, Mrs Nicholls," the Duke responded.

At this, Roberta laughed slightly.

"It's 'Miss', actually!"

"Oh, I do apologise!"

"Anyway, if you'd just kindly like to step this way, we'll show you to your seat," said Alan.

The Duke stepped up into the carriage and made his way to his

First Class seat before Alan and Roberta followed. Alan sat opposite the Duke, next to Eric, while Roberta rejoined Jane in the buffet car. Richard Davidson had been informed of the presence of their important guest, and the need to drive as smoothly as possible!

Once the train was ready to leave, Derek blew his whistle and waved his flag and the train began to move. In the buffet car, Jane and Roberta began to make breakfast for the passengers, taking extra care with the Duke's. Despite the additional pressure, all the train crew felt highly privileged to be in the presence of their local dignitary, and were determined to do their utmost to impress him.

After the train reached Wrexham, Alan started explaining how the service had started. Eric and the Duke both thought it was quite remarkable that it had managed to attract sufficient custom to keep running for so long, when there was a much faster service from Liverpool. The way it had helped to revitalise New Brighton so much was also of great interest to the Duke; he had helped breathe a lot of new life into Liverpool himself by funding the Liverpool One shopping development.

"That's really made a very big difference to the city centre. Some parts of it were getting terribly run down and dilapidated," said Alan, once the conversation had turned to this subject.

"It certainly has," agreed Eric.

At this point, Roberta approached carrying plates of breakfast for the three men. She happened to overhear the men talking about the general safety of Liverpool City Centre and how it was a lot different to its stereotypical reputation. She was surprised when the Duke told them that his two daughters had once said they felt safer in the centre of Liverpool at night than in the centre of Chester!

"That's remarkable!" she exclaimed.

"Well, Chester can get quite rough at night, believe it or not," replied Alan.

"Some people can find that quite surprising," said the Duke. "But you're quite right."

The rest of the journey passed without incident, the train making its usual stops from Wrexham to Banbury. It stopped for much longer than usual at Shrewsbury in order to give Richard a break – at this point they would normally have changed drivers, but the desire to provide as smooth a journey as possible for the Duke had resulted in Richard being chosen to undertake the entire journey by himself, due to his prestigious skill in driving gently. As with most charter trains, the journey was somewhat slower because the ordinary service trains were always given priority on the line ahead. Plenty of time had been built into the schedule to allow for this.

Between Banbury and Marylebone, an additional stop was made at Wembley Stadium, where the Port Sunlight Players were to alight and take their props and equipment with them. Derek and Stuart carefully unloaded the boxes and helped the troupe to move them out of the station. The cast and equipment would then be taken to the theatre where they were to perform, while the train continued to its final destination of Marylebone, where the rest of the passengers would disembark.

That evening, the Mersey2Marylebone staff again attended the performance of the play. Like the first performance in Port Sunlight, they had a most enjoyable time and thought it made a great deal of difference to see the production in a much bigger theatre.

CHAPTER 11

QUEENS AND RUGBY

The following year would be another big event in Liverpool. To celebrate the 175th anniversary of Cunard, the company's 'Three Queens' would all be visiting the city at the same time. The *Queen Mary 2* would be returning, but this time would be accompanied by her two sister ships, the *Queen Victoria* and the *Queen Elizabeth*. Like the *QM2*'s first visit, Mersey2Marylebone saw this as yet another excellent opportunity for more business – and they weren't disappointed!

As before, the stops that normally only picked up in the London direction and set down in the other were made into full station stops for that day. However, with Merseyrail services now able to run to New Brighton from the Borderlands Line, there wasn't the same need for this. During the afternoon, some of the train crew found time to observe the three ships from the seafront in New Brighton; the *QM2* was tied up at the landing stage and the other two anchored in mid-river.

"It's such a spectacular sight!" remarked Stuart.

"Yeah, very much so," agreed Jane.

"We should feel very privileged, seeing the Queen Elizabeth!" joked Derek.

"Yeah, just a pity it's the one that floats instead of the one that has a crown on her head!"

"Well, next year is when she's due to become our longest-reigning monarch. I dare say there'll be plenty of events to commemorate that!"

"Will they have to rename stations called 'Victoria' as a result?" asked Roberta.

"Hmm… somehow, I don't think asking for a Day Return to Manchester Elizabeth has quite the same ring to it!" Alan replied, amused.

They all laughed.

Two months later, England was due to host the Rugby World Cup, and Alan announced that – like the Olympics 3 years earlier – Mersey2Marylebone would be running additional services for the duration of the tournament to take people to and from matches in London.

"Oh no!" groaned Roberta, thinking back to the specials they had run for the FA Cup tie.

"Don't worry," Jane reassured. "Rugby supporters tend to be more civilised than football ones, strangely enough!"

"Yeah," added Alan. "They say that rugby is a game for hooligans played by gentlemen, whereas football is a game for gentlemen played by hooligans!"

Luke found this highly amusing.

"Really? I always thought rugby stood for Remarkably Unattractive Gentlemen Behaving Yobbishly!" he joked.

The first service was designed to coincide with the opening match of the competition at Twickenham, and it was very well patronised by passionate rugby fans from all over North Wales. Anticipating extra passengers due to the huge popularity of the sport among the Welsh people, the train had been scheduled to make additional stops between Shotton and Shrewsbury to pick up as many of them as possible.

The trains continued to be well used throughout the World Cup and, as Jane had assured Roberta, the supporters were generally a lot less rowdy than the football ones who had travelled to the FA Cup tie!

On the day of the final, the train was more crowded than ever. The decision to introduce a permanent service from Birkenhead was to prove a very good one, since this had meant the trains being longer once south of Wrexham. The result was extra capacity for the hordes of people travelling to the match. Mersey2Marylebone had already had some experience of transporting Welsh rugby fans whenever England and Wales had met at Twickenham during the Six Nations, but never on this scale.

In the weeks following the World Cup, Alan began to feel very pleased with how well the service had lasted. The concerns about whether they could succeed where Wrexham & Shropshire had failed now seemed a distant memory. The following year brought with it more events to mark the Queen becoming the longest-reigning British monarch of all time. This, in turn, meant more business.

At times he couldn't help thinking – what had he been worried about?

The End

ABOUT THE AUTHOR

Philip Ion was born in 1987 on the Wirral, Merseyside. He was educated at St Werburgh's RC Primary School in Birkenhead and later at Our Lady of Pity RC Primary School in Greasby (Wirral), followed by Woodchurch High School and Birkenhead Sixth Form College. He subsequently obtained an Honours degree in Chemistry from the University of Liverpool.

He was diagnosed at an early age with Asperger's Syndrome. People with this lifelong condition, although often highly intelligent, can often find it very difficult to express themselves clearly and communicate effectively with others. They see the world around them rather differently from most of us, and need support and understanding to help them to relate successfully to their fellow human beings. However, if this is forthcoming, it can often be the key to unlocking rich potential in such people; empowering them to make a full and effective contribution to daily life, and enabling them to take their rightful place as valued and respected members of society.

Philip has always been interested in railways. He made his first rail journey at the age of three on the Severn Valley Railway, and since those days he has travelled extensively by train both in the UK and abroad. He has visited many of the preserved railways in Britain, and has been fascinated by their history and the story of their restoration from abandoned and overgrown track-beds to fully working operations – some of which are beginning once again to provide public services as well as leisure experiences.

The vision, skill, commitment and sheer hard work of the countless volunteers who are the backbone of the railway preservation movement in Britain and elsewhere has been a source of immense pride for Philip, and has inspired him to write this collection of short stories to honour their achievements. Each story is a fictional tale, but is based on historical facts and events. Each reflects Philip's boundless enthusiasm for railways, the pleasure they give to so many ordinary people like himself, and the part they can play in the modern world. Each speaks in different ways of triumph over adversity, and reflects Philip's own experience of coming to terms with the realities of life and his appreciation that success needs hard work, can never be guaranteed – and is therefore all the sweeter when it comes.

This book is not only a celebration of our railway heritage and those who by their efforts transform it into a combination of living history and modern utility for the benefit of future generations. It is a testament to Philip's determination to overcome the difficulties of self-expression that at one point threatened to deprive him of the GCSE Grade C in English Language that he needed in order to go to University. It is also a tribute to the dedication and professionalism of all those teachers, support staff and clinicians who tutored and cared for Philip throughout his school and University career, to the far-sightedness of Wirral Metropolitan Borough Council who provided the specialist facilities and resources to help him to fulfill his educational potential, and most of all to the unfailing love and support of his devoted family.